"Maybe single parents like us ought to team up?"

He turned so quickly at her words, he felt a crick in his neck. "What?"

She bit her lip. "Combine skill sets. Conserve our resources. Divide and conquer."

His heart hammered. What was she suggesting?

"The care and feeding of adolescents, remember? We can help each other." Kristina blushed. "You're helping me with my fear of flying. I can help you with your fear of parenting."

When he didn't say anything—he wasn't sure what to say—she fretted at the hem of her sweater. "Gray told me most of your dusting takes place in the early morning. I could do morning car pool, and you could do afternoon pickup."

"Share the load?"

"Exactly. Besides, Gray is hungry for a positive male influence."

Canyon wasn't sure he qualified for that title. On the other hand, did he need a reason to justify wanting to spend more time with the intriguing widow? If he did, she'd offered him one on a silver platter.

Only a fool would refuse such an opportunity.

Lisa Carter and her family make their home in North Carolina. In addition to her Love Inspired novels, she writes romantic suspense for Abingdon Press. When she isn't writing, Lisa enjoys traveling to romantic locales, teaching writing workshops and researching her next exotic adventure. She has strong opinions on barbecue and ACC basketball. She loves to hear from readers. Connect with Lisa at lisacarterauthor.com.

Books by Lisa Carter

Love Inspired

Coast Guard Courtship
Coast Guard Sweetheart
Falling for the Single Dad
The Deputy's Perfect Match
The Bachelor's Unexpected Family

The Bachelor's Unexpected Family

Lisa Carter

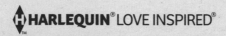

Recycling programs
for this product may
not exist in your area.

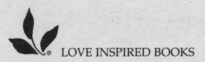

® LOVE INSPIRED BOOKS

ISBN-13: 978-0-373-62300-6

The Bachelor's Unexpected Family

www.Harlequin.com

Printed in U.S.A.

Brethren, I do not regard myself as having laid hold of it yet; but one thing I do: forgetting what lies behind and reaching forward to what lies ahead, I press on toward the goal for the prize of the upward call of God in Christ Jesus.
—*Philippians* 3:13–14

Dedicated to the memory of my late stepfather,
Thomas W. Fulghum. Thank you
for being my mother's second chance at love.
And thank you for giving your heart
to a Jade like me. I miss you still.

Chapter One

There it was again. Kristina Montgomery frowned at the faint whining noise above the treetops. Same as yesterday.

Leaning over the sink at the kitchen window, her gaze shifted to the sky. A small plane hovered above the tree line rimming her property. The yellow wings floated like a bright golden bird in the morning sunlight.

A robin called a cheery greeting from the winter-stark branches of a nearby oak. The droning of bees filled the air above the overgrown bushes, heirloom roses, which would burst into fragrant bloom come spring.

Provided spring ever came. Since her husband died two years ago, she'd felt trapped in her own stark winter of grief.

She'd bought the 1930s Arts and Crafts bungalow because of those rosebushes. And for the neglected garden.

Why? Maybe because of the inherent promise of new beginnings the garden held for her and her son. She and Gray had desperately needed a new beginning.

She scowled at the mechanical bird, a painful reminder of everything she'd lost. If she'd known the property adjoined a private airfield, she would've never purchased the run-down place.

In the twenty-six months since Pax's death, she'd ridden a roller coaster of extreme emotion. She was caught somehow between overwhelming grief and a paralyzing fear of how she was going to raise their son alone.

At the edge of the woods separating her peaceful sanctuary from the airstrip, she spotted her son's bike. She blew out a breath. How many times had she told him not to go over there? The airplane dipped one wing before disappearing beyond the forested horizon.

Gray had promised—she'd made him promise—to stay away from the airfield. But she should've recognized the stubborn glint in his brown eyes. The same glint her husband used to get every time he got into a cockpit.

Until above a windswept Afghan mountain, a rocket-propelled grenade had slammed into his plane. Hurling Pax and his fighter jet into a thousand pieces of jagged, burning metal—

She sucked in a breath and closed her eyes against the images that played in her dreams every night. Her hand tightened around the dangling chain of her husband's dog tags. She had to stop doing this. She had to move on, for Gray's sake. Mired in the past, she was no good to her son.

Her head throbbed. She rubbed her temples. Like father, like son? Her eyes flew open.

She refused to allow history to repeat itself. Not with her son. Not with the only person she had left.

Tucking the dog tags inside the collar of her pink shirt, she thrust open the screen door. The hinges screeched. She dashed down the concrete steps. The door slammed behind her. In dress flats for her morning meeting, she stalked across the grass toward the trees.

Sidestepping the bike, she followed a faded trail toward their very unwelcome neighbor. The overhanging tree canopy blocked most of the sunlight. She shivered and wrapped the open ends of her brown cardigan around herself.

February on the Eastern Shore of Virginia was much too cold to go outside without a coat. Knowing Gray, he was most likely in shirtsleeves.

She picked her way across the pine-needled footpath

and emerged into a paved clearing to find the plane, wheels down, at the end of the runway. Engine roaring and propellers whirring, the pilot taxied the golden-yellow plane toward the terminal.

A metallic, tin-roofed hangar and a small brick building anchored the beginning of the runway. Beside the hangar, a sign—Wallace & Collier Crop Aviation Specialists.

Great. Just great. Somehow of all the houses for sale on the Delmarva Peninsula, she'd managed to buy the one next door to a barnstorming, daredevil crop duster.

Her teenage son waved at the plane as it rolled forward. But when he caught sight of her, his hand quickly dropped to his side.

"You got that right, buster. You're in big trouble," she muttered under her breath. And without stopping to think, she charged across the runway toward him. Gray's eyes widened.

"Mom! Watch out. Get out of the way!"

Too late, she realized she'd stepped into the path of the oncoming plane. She froze. The sound of the propeller filled her ears.

Gray raced across the runway. Grabbing her arm, he yanked her out of the way. The pilot braked and swerved. The plane skidded as the wheels struggled for traction before finally shuddering to a stop.

Falling onto the grassy area, Gray took the brunt of the impact. But with the resilience of youth, he sprang to his feet.

She rose slowly, feeling every bit of her thirty-eight years. "Gray, honey, are you—"

"What were you thinking, Mom?" Hands on his skinny hips, he gestured to the plane. "Walking in front of a moving aircraft? Seriously?"

Shoving open the cockpit door, the pilot emerged. In

jeans and work boots, his flannel shirtsleeves rolled to his elbows, he clambered out and dropped to the asphalt.

A baseball cap obscured the upper portion of his face. But there was no mistaking the taut anger whipstitching his mouth, nor his jutting jaw as he advanced. "What kind of idiot walks into the path of an airplane?" he yelled.

She bristled. Pilots, the same the world over. Civilian or military, lords of the universe. Or so they believed.

Gray's mouth went mulish. "Thanks a lot, Mom. Now Canyon's going to kick me out of here for good."

"You have no business being here." She wagged her finger in his face. "Not after we talked. We agreed."

Why was Pax not here to help her parent Gray during the rebellious teen years?

Gray crossed his arms over his seen-better-days T-shirt. "You talked, Mom. I agreed to nothing."

He widened his stance to hip width. An airman's stance. Her breath hitched at the uncanny resemblance to his late father.

Kristina's heart pounded at the memory of the last time she'd seen Pax—not knowing she'd never see him again. This couldn't happen to Gray. Not to her only child.

"You don't belong here, Gray."

The infuriated pilot arrived at the tail end of her words. "You want to talk about having no business here, lady?"

She stiffened. "A mother has a right to keep her child out of harm's way."

"Only one in harm's way today was me." The pilot lifted the ball cap off his head and slapped it against his thigh. "After you almost crashed my plane."

She took her first good look at her unwanted neighbor.

Late thirties. Classic, high cheekbones. A long Roman nose. His jaw dark with beard stubble. A strong brow. Curly brown hair.

His eyes flashed. An electric blue, in a face tanned by

the sun and wind. Something fluttered like a swirl of butterfly wings in the pit of her stomach. Something she hadn't experienced since meeting another brash young airman during a long-ago church softball game.

With a sense of betraying that now dead young man, remorse blanketed her. Her hand automatically drifted to the chain underneath her shirt collar. And she stuffed the unwelcome feelings into a dark corner of her heart. For good measure, she glowered at the Eastern Shore pilot.

At the motion of her hand, he narrowed his eyes. Lines crinkled the corners of his eyes. Lines that probably feathered when he smiled. Which he wasn't doing now.

Handsome by anyone's definition. And from his body language, as arrogant and cocky as they came. She ought to know.

Once upon a time, she'd married one.

Canyon didn't miss the scorn on her face. *Welcome to Kiptohanock to you, too, neighbor.*

Not seeing a car in the office parking space, he figured she'd walked over through the woods from next door. Gray must take after his father. The boy's dark features didn't resemble the woman. She could've been a cover model for a Scandinavian travel brochure.

Or considering her frosty demeanor, Icelandic. Although, if he remembered rightly, Greenland was the one with most of the glaciers.

"Which one are you?" She flicked her hand toward the sign. "Wallace or Collier?"

"Collier." He jerked his thumb in the direction of her house. "And which one are you?"

Her chin came up. "I'm the woman who would've never bought this property if I knew we were in the flight path of your crop duster."

One of those genteel, upper-crust Southern voices. Not

the nowhere accent of Northern Virginia. Nor the twang of the Blue Ridge. Probably from central Virginia or the Carolinas.

He tightened his jaw. "I'm an aerial application specialist. And I've been careful to not fly over your house."

"Mom..." Gray tugged at her sleeve. "Stop embarrassing me. Canyon is my boss."

She planted one hand on her jeans-clad hip. "As if I'd ever allow you to work for a sky jockey like him."

Canyon's eyebrows rose. Interesting turn of phrase. He hadn't heard that one since his Coast Guard days.

"Especially after what happened to your father."

Without meaning to, Canyon's eyes cut to the bare space on her left hand. A widow? A silver chain half-hidden in the folds of her collar glinted. Had Gray's father been an airline fatality?

As for his first impression of Gray's mother? Tall, a willowy five foot eight, Canyon estimated, to his six-foot height. Long, wavy blond hair spilled over her thin shoulders. Classic oval features. Fair skinned. And her eyes?

Her eyes gave Canyon pause. His grandmother would've called her eyes china blue. Like the blue in a field of cornflowers.

Those eyes sent an inexplicable pang through his heart. A yearning for something to which he'd believed himself immune.

According to the real estate papers he'd signed at closing, this must be K. Montgomery. Since the attorney had handled everything, he'd assumed the new owner was a man and that Gray, who'd started hanging out at the airfield a few weeks ago, the man's son. But the disturbing, angry woman was definitely not a man.

Canyon folded his arms across his chest. He'd sold his grandmother's house to buy the Air Tractor 802 he just landed. Landed safely, no thanks to K. Montgomery. His misfortune to sell what little remained of his family heritage to an aircraft hater.

He shrugged. "I invited Gray to help me out on the repair of an engine. The boy likes to tinker."

K. Montgomery's china-blue eyes became chips of sapphire. "The boy is my fifteen-year-old son. He doesn't have my permission to work here. An airfield is dangerous. I ought to report you for child endangerment."

"My mistake, lady." When would he learn? In his experience, no good deed ever went unpunished. "The boy looks sixteen. Won't happen again."

Gray inserted himself between them. "Canyon was doing me a favor. Teaching me how to repair engines. I like being here."

The woman squared her shoulders. "I absolutely will not allow you to put your life at risk."

Gray went rigid. "Moving here was supposed to be about making a new start for both of us. But since Dad died, all you care about is making me miserable. As miserable as you."

"I'm not—" She pursed her lips. "Being around airplanes will only make you feel worse, Gray."

Gray held his ground. "Just because you're afraid of airplanes doesn't mean I have to hate them, too. It makes me happy to remember Dad here. You're the one who makes me feel sad."

Canyon angled toward Gray's mother. "Your son's a really good kid. Your husband would be proud. And I'd never put Gray in harm's way. He's good company."

The woman blinked at him for a moment.

Canyon scrubbed his hand over his face. Bothered— strangely—that he'd forgotten to shave this morning. Bothered, too, that he was fighting so hard to keep the boy working at the airfield.

She faced Gray. "Go back to the house. I won't risk losing you the way we lost your father." She glared at Canyon. "And I'm *not* afraid of airplanes."

Gray snorted. "You're afraid of everything since Dad died. Afraid to laugh. Afraid to live. And I'm sick of living in the grave with you."

Hurt flitted across her features.

An unusual—and unwelcome—sensation of protectiveness rose in Canyon's chest. "Just a minute, Gray…"

Gray's brown eyes darkened. "You don't know what it's like. She won't let me do anything because she's afraid I'll get hurt." His shoulders hunched. "Stop treating me like a baby, Mom."

"Then stop acting like one, Gray," Canyon growled.

Gray flushed.

Canyon sighed. How had he gotten entangled in this quicksand? Since leaving the Coast Guard, he'd spent the last three years making sure he stayed out of other people's business and that people stayed out of his.

He took a breath. "What does the K stand for?"

"Kristina." Gray kicked a loose stone on the concrete. "I like working with motors, Mom. And Canyon needs my help." Gray leaned forward. "Tell her, Canyon. Tell her how much you need my help."

Kristina Montgomery's lovely face hardened. "Your only job is school, Gray."

Gray clenched his hands. "Since you don't have a job, I figure maybe I better."

Canyon's brow puckered. "I didn't realize you were looking for work. What do you do?"

She opened her mouth, but once again Gray beat her to the punch.

"Mom cuts great triangle sandwiches." Gray's mouth twisted. "She has a green thumb. And can clean a toilet like nobody's business."

She quivered at his sarcasm.

Canyon had had enough of the attitude. "Let's you and me get one thing straight right now, Grayson Montgomery. I will not tolerate disrespect to any woman, much less your mother."

Gray's and his mother's gazes swung to Canyon's.

"She cares about you or she wouldn't have come looking for you. Good mothers don't grow on trees. I should know."

Canyon grimaced. What on earth had possessed him to share that little tidbit from his less-than-stellar childhood?

Her cheeks heated. "I apologize for my son's extreme rudeness." She swallowed. "And to answer your question, I have an accounting degree from the University of Richmond that I've never used."

Canyon recalled only one other person on the Eastern Shore originally from Richmond. "Any relation to Weston Clark? The ex-Coast Guard commander who remodeled the old lighthouse on the Neck?"

"He's my brother."

Canyon noted the likeness then. Weston Clark had been married for not quite a year to one of the Duer girls—Caroline. Those girls had been a few years behind Canyon in high school. Closer to Beech's age.

The thought of his brother put Canyon's stomach in knots. He didn't have time for this altercation with Kristina Montgomery. He still had a ton of stuff to get done before he met Jade and the social worker at the bus depot in Exmore.

He crimped the brim of his cap. "I can't allow you to work here without your mom's permission."

Gray sputtered. "B-but she's being unfair."

Canyon shook his head. "Nevertheless, she's your mother, and she gets to call the shots."

"I have an appointment in Kiptohanock." Kristina Montgomery swept a curtain of blond hair out of her face. "And I meant what I said, Gray. Go home."

The boy's countenance fell. "But—"

"Do what your mother says, Gray."

Gray threw his mother and Canyon an angry look before he stomped toward the wooded path. Kristina Montgomery remained rooted in place, watching her son.

"I run a clean, safe enterprise, Mrs. Montgomery. Let me take you on a short flight and give you a bird's eye view of the Shore."

Canyon bit the inside of his cheek. *Where had that come from?*

Her forehead creased. Gray's mother didn't appear to smile much. Maybe she hadn't had a reason to smile in a long while.

"Thanks, but no thanks. I don't trust airplanes." She moved to follow her son.

"Nor pilots, either, from the sound of it."

She stopped.

"One word of advice, Mrs. Montgomery?"

She crossed her arms but waited to hear him out.

"If you refuse to let Gray pursue an interest he obviously loves, you might be the one risking everything."

Her mouth flattened. "What are you talking about, Mr. Collier?"

"My name's Canyon. And I'm talking about risking your relationship with your son. You could lose him for good."

She tilted her head. "And you, I assume, are an expert on parenting? Why do you care?"

"Just being neighborly, ma'am."

Which was so not true. He must be lonelier than he'd believed. Though after Jade arrived today, loneliness was sure to be less of a factor.

"Let me give *you* a piece of advice, Canyon Collier." She jabbed her index finger in the space between them. "Mind your own business."

Exactly what he thought he'd been doing. Until a certain blonde widow walked into the path of his incoming plane.

Pivoting on her heel, she trudged toward the woods without giving him a backward glance. And, discomfited, Canyon couldn't for the life of him figure what *had* gotten into him.

Chapter Two

The tangy scent of sea salt filled Kristina's nostrils as she rolled down the car window. In the sky above the rocky point of the lighthouse beach, a gull screeched and performed an acrobatic figure eight.

Weston emerged from the keeper's cottage and sauntered to the car. "Hey, big sis. How's life treating you?"

His elder by a mere eighteen months, her mouth quirked. "Where's your beautiful wife?"

As if on cue, the door opened. Caroline and ten-year-old Izzie spilled out into the milky sunshine of the late February morning.

Married life looked good on her brother. After a disastrous first marriage to a woman who deserted her brother and baby Izzie, Weston had found a new life and love on Virginia's Eastern Shore.

Kristina fought a stab of envy. She'd never begrudge her brother his hard-won happiness, but that didn't stop her from longing for a new life of her own. As for love?

She'd buried her chance for love when they lowered Pax's coffin into the earth at Arlington National Cemetery.

Weston propped his elbows on the window. "Thanks for taking Caroline into Kiptohanock. The completion of the marine animal rescue center is at a critical juncture, and with her car on the fritz..."

"No problem. Opening day still set for May?"

He grinned. "If my beloved aquatic veterinarian wife has anything to say about it, then yes."

Redheaded Izzie launched herself at the open window. "Hey, Aunt Kristina."

"Well, if it isn't my favorite niece." Kristina winked. "Hey, yourself."

Izzie giggled. "I'm your only niece, Aunt Kristina."

Auburn-haired Caroline nudged aside her husband with her hip. "I hate to further impose, but could we drop off Izz at my sister Amelia's house? With today being a teacher workday…"

Weston made a face. "And I'm on deadline with an engineering project for a Baltimore client."

Kristina held up her hand. "Say no more. Gray's moping at my house, too."

Of course, he hadn't moped until she grounded him for sneaking over to the airfield.

"You need me to bring them home, Wes?"

Weston rapped a beat with his palms on the car door. "I'll finish in time to bring my girls home."

His girls. Kristina bit back a sigh. She'd been loved like that once.

Izzie hugged her dad goodbye. "Maybe Gray could come play with Max and me."

Max—Caroline's nephew and all-around Kiptohanock mischief maker. Gray would consider being left with a bunch of ten-year-olds nothing short of babysitting.

Caroline smoothed a strand of Izzie's hair. "I'm sure Gray has high school stuff to do, ladybug."

The little girl chattered nonstop until they dropped her off at the Dutch-roof farmhouse Max's dad, Braeden Scott—commander of the Kiptohanock Coast Guard station—had recently purchased for his growing family.

Kristina's hands tightened on the wheel. With Gray usually at school, time moved in slow motion for her. Too often leaving her feeling without purpose and alone.

She cleared her throat. "You've made my brother and Izzie so happy, Caroline. Thank you."

"My pleasure entirely." A sweet smile curved Caroline's lips. "They've made *me* so happy."

Happiness seemed forever out of reach for Kristina.

"There've been adjustments." Caroline stashed her purse on the floorboard beside her foot. "A good marriage requires work." She raised her gaze to meet Kristina's. "You know how it is. Letting go of the past with its fears and building something new together. Hard, but good work."

Letting go of the fear... Kristina's problem in a clamshell.

She slowed the car as they approached the town limits of oceanside Kiptohanock. "Including throwing my lovable but high-energy niece into the equation, too."

Caroline smiled. "Life is never dull with Izzie. I wouldn't have it any other way. Nothing worth keeping is ever easy. But in the long run, a risk so worth taking."

Relationships. Risk. Was that arrogant crop duster— aerial application specialist—correct? Was Kristina risking her relationship with her son because of fear?

She steered the vehicle toward the waterfront. The town librarian passed the gazebo on the village green. Caroline threw out her hand in greeting.

"Evy Pruitt," Caroline added by way of explanation. "Newly married to Deputy Sheriff Charlie Pruitt."

After years of moving from one base to the next, Kristina loved the small-town friendliness. "Evy's also Sawyer Kole's sister, right? And therefore your other sister Honey's sister-in-law. Got it."

Which in the hospitable South made the young librarian not only kin by marriage to Caroline, but in a weirdly, endearing kind of way kin to Kristina, too.

Bypassing the Sandpiper Café and the Coast Guard station, Kristina nosed the car into a parking space along the seawall outside the former seafood-processing building. Power tools buzzed as the renovations on the aquatic center neared completion.

Caroline opened the door. "Thanks, Kristina."

"Before you go…"

Caroline paused, one foot on the ground.

Kristina took a breath. "I wondered if you might have heard anything about the crop—" She moistened her lips. "I mean, the aerial application specialist out my way. Canyon Collier."

Caroline's brown eyes narrowed. "What has he done? Is he bothering you? If so, Weston will—"

"It's not that. Collier offered Gray a part-time job at the airfield, and I wanted to find out more before I agreed."

"He and his brother were ahead of me by a few grades in high school." Caroline's eyes dropped to her shoes. "And we didn't run in the same circles."

Kristina's lips tightened. "By your tone, I'm sensing their circles ran toward trouble."

Caroline let out a breath. "I'm the last person in the world to cast stones, but one of the Colliers got into big trouble back then. I don't remember which brother."

Kristina's heart thumped. "You mean trouble with the law?"

"Like I said, I don't remember which brother. They left the Shore soon after. By force or choice, I don't know. One went into the Coast Guard, though."

Kristina assumed that would be Canyon Collier. Maybe where he acquired his aviation skills.

"I don't know much about the one who returned." Caroline cocked her head. "Given my own history of being a black sheep prodigal, I'm inclined to give him the benefit of the doubt."

"Whether he deserves it or not?"

Caroline nodded. "Whether he deserves it or not. But by all accounts, this Collier has built a solid agribusiness with the local farmers. A good pilot, I've heard. A trustworthy businessman."

"But what about Gray working there?" Kristina bit her lip. "This job and this guy have become important to Gray."

Uncomfortably important to her son. But if she were honest, she was equally disturbed by the fluttery feeling the man had evoked in her as well.

Caroline turned toward the whine of a drill inside the building. "You should talk to Evy's brother, Sawyer. He's the general contractor on the renovation. I've seen him and Collier hanging out at the Sandpiper over Long John doughnuts."

Or maybe it would also be wise to talk to Evy Pruitt's deputy sheriff husband.

Caroline unfolded from the car. "And of course, you must pray about what to do."

Kristina's gaze skittered to the white clapboard church whose steeple brushed the sky above the harbor. How could she tell her sister-in-law that since Pax died, her prayers felt as if they bounced off a Teflon ceiling?

Where was God when Pax was killed? Had God been off duty when she was widowed? What kind of Father would leave Gray without a father?

But she couldn't say those things to Caroline, whose own rediscovered faith had been wrested from a dark abyss of despair. Kristina fidgeted in her seat at her blasphemous thoughts. She'd been raised to put her trust and hope in God.

Which was exactly the problem. Her trust had been shattered and her hope as lost as Pax's plane. Even worse, she didn't know how to get them back. And she wasn't unaware that her faith had ebbed at the same rate the fear had taken hold.

Caroline closed the car door with a soft click. "Everyone deserves a second chance, Kristina. I'm so thankful God gave me a do-over, despite the bad choices I made in the past."

Everyone deserved a second chance. Until they didn't. Kristina backed out of the parking space. Did that include her, too?

Canyon wrapped his hands around the steering wheel of the Jeep Cherokee. The tension was palpable enough to cut with a propeller. He shot a furtive look at the sixteen-year-old girl beside him.

Shoulders hunched, Jade stared out the window at the passing scenery. She was no longer the little girl he remembered. But then, he'd last laid eyes on her almost a decade ago.

He should've tried harder. With a mother like Jade's, he should've kept in touch. But keeping in touch meant entangling complications. Cords binding him to a past he'd rather forget. Snares he thought he'd left behind when he ditched the Shore after high school and enlisted in the Coast Guard.

Canyon rubbed his hand over his face. Jade swiveled. They locked eyes for a moment.

The vulnerability in her green eyes punched him in the gut. The fear in her gaze, however, was swiftly replaced by the all too familiar anger Jade wore like a cloak around her thin shoulders. For Canyon, guilt surged anew.

How had he let himself get talked into the guardianship of a belligerent adolescent he barely recognized? Kristina Montgomery had hit the nail on the head earlier—what did he know about parenting?

Especially parenting a teenage girl. This was going to

be a disaster. None of this ought to be his responsibility. He let out a sigh.

"This isn't something either you or I wanted." Jade waved her hand. "Take me to the ferry. I'll go to the mainland. Child Protective Services will be none the wiser."

He gripped the wheel. "And exactly how do you think you'd survive alone over there?"

"Just like I fended for myself before getting nabbed by the police."

"You were arrested because you broke the law by shoplifting, Jade."

Those green eyes of hers smoldered. "It was a pack of beef jerky."

"Why did you do it, Jade? To prove you could? For a dare?"

"I—I…" She turned to the window. "I was hungry. Brandi had spent her paycheck, and I hadn't seen her in a week."

Another punch to his solar plexus. He could only imagine how Brandi—Jade's so-called mother—had spent the meager salary she earned at the Gas and Go Quick Stop. At the image of Jade on the streets alone, something inside him twisted.

Far too reminiscent of what had happened to him and Jade's father, Beech, before their mom dropped them off at their grandma's in Kiptohanock and did everyone a favor by never coming back.

"I guarantee you won't go hungry." His voice was gruff. "But like it or not, you're stuck with me, kid."

From the set expression on her face, he concluded she liked it about as much as him. Still, he was supposed to be the grown-up.

"It's going to be all right, Jade."

She snorted. "Since when has anything ever been right for Colliers?"

And that—he heaved another sigh—was the long and short of it.

When he pulled off the highway onto Seaside Road, he gave her the ten-cent tour of town. Circling the square with the gazebo, he pointed out all-important landmarks like the library.

She tossed her long black, magenta-streaked hair over her shoulder. "I don't read."

"You mean you don't like to read."

Rounding one side of the square, he gestured to the church.

Prompting a churlish sneer from Jade. "So not happening."

He felt a surge of churlishness coming on himself. "You'll do what I tell you to do, Jade."

Which was about as effective as when his grandmother used to lay down the law for him and Beech. His grandmother had been right about church, though. It hadn't hurt him.

"It's a good way to get to know others your age in the community."

Jade gave him a nice view of her back and didn't bother to reply.

Fighting for patience, he pointed out the Coast Guard station, where flags fluttered. Recreational and commercial fishing boats bobbed in the harbor. He pulled into an empty space in front of the Sandpiper Café and cut the engine.

"Why are we stopping?"

"For the famous Long John doughnuts. They're the best."

She glared. "I repeat, why are we stopping?"

He reminded himself for the hundredth time since the social worker had called last week, he was the adult. And he needed to act like one.

Canyon rested his arms on the steering wheel. "This is where the locals hang out. This is where you get to redefine yourself, Jade. It's a pretty little town. With lots of great people."

"The same people who ran you and Beech out of town."

He'd never once heard Jade call Beech *father*. Canyon knew enough to realize his feckless younger sibling had never earned the title.

"I came back because it's a good place to live." He let his shoulders rise and fall. "It's the closest to home this Collier could find."

Again, Jade curled her lip. "And courtesy of the Accomack County Sheriff's Department, Beech found his new home in prison."

"That was Beech's own doing, Jade. I wouldn't like to see you travel the same path. Kiptohanock is your chance for a new beginning."

"Since when does anybody give Colliers like us second chances?"

Hardheadedness apparently being an unfortunate Collier family trait.

Canyon raked his hand over his head. "That's exactly what I'm giving you, Jade. A chance to start over. You can be anything you want to be. Choose to be smarter than the rest of us sooner. How about doughnuts and a Coca-Cola float?"

He had it on good authority—his friend Sawyer Kole, ex-Coastie and now happily married father of five-month-old Daisy—that all kids loved ice cream and sugar.

But Jade refused to get out of the Jeep.

He gritted his teeth. Sawyer better enjoy his precious baby girl, because Canyon had news for him—parenting promised to only get rockier from there.

Exasperated, he swung open the car door. "More for me then."

If this was a sign of things to come, it was going to be a long two years until she turned eighteen.

He moved toward the glass-fronted diner. Who was he kidding? He and Jade would be fortunate to survive together till Easter.

And his eyes flickered toward the cross atop the steeple. Jade—not the Coast Guard or flying airplanes—might make a praying man out of him yet.

Chapter Three

Hands folded in her lap, Kristina glanced around the ladies' parlor at the members of the church altar guild. She wasn't sure why she'd come to the Easter planning meeting this morning. But while living the vagabond life of a military wife, she'd often longed for a place to establish roots.

Especially for Gray. He hadn't been the type of child who adjusted well to a new school every few years. Bookish, a video geek, he didn't make friends easily.

Nor did she. It was simpler not to reach out. Or face the inevitable sorrow of parting with friends when Pax was restationed.

But this time she wanted things to be different. This was a new start for them. Kiptohanock, a place to make a real home. After Pax died, she'd moved across the country to the Shore to be near Weston.

The Eastern Shore of Virginia was a narrow peninsula separating the Chesapeake Bay from the Atlantic Ocean. Isolated. Not as readily accessible to the rest of the continental United States.

Her grandfather had been the last lighthouse keeper before the Coast Guard decommissioned the lighthouse in the 1950s. But her family had returned each summer. She possessed fond memories of those idyllic beach days and wanted Gray to know the same.

Small-town life. A caring community. After a lifetime of following Pax around the world.

Here, Gray had a chance to know what it meant to be part of a close-knit family. To watch summer fireflies. To clam. To fish. Before he left her forever.

So when she read the announcement in the church bulletin inviting anyone interested in serving on the altar guild to attend a planning meeting, she'd decided to give it a try. To make new friends. To get involved in community life.

Now she wasn't so sure. The encounter with Canyon Collier had left her feeling oddly exposed. She shrugged off the vague feelings of vulnerability. Anyone would be shaken after almost being run over by an airplane. And she pushed the incident to the nether regions of her mind.

Her gaze traveled over the ladies at the meeting. Sixty-something Mrs. Davenport held court in a brocade armchair strategically placed at the unofficial head of the room. According to Caroline, Mrs. Davenport was a social force to be reckoned with in Kiptohanock.

Librarian Evy Pruitt perched in a nearby chair. The pastor's wife, Agnes Parks, smiled at Kristina while Mrs. Davenport waxed on about Lenten altar cloths. And there was also Caroline's sister, Honey Kole. She owned the Duer Fisherman's Lodge. Her darling baby daughter dozed in her car seat on the carpet at Honey's feet.

Kristina bit off a sigh. She'd always wanted more children. But Pax had been deployed so often that he thought after Gray was born, one child was enough.

Honey played with the pearls at her throat. "What about breakfast after the Easter sunrise service?"

The other ladies hid their smiles behind teacups. And Kristina got the distinct impression if anyone was likely to challenge Mrs. Davenport's leadership, Honey Duer Kole might be the one to do it.

Which was fine. Kristina had no social aspirations. By nature, she was more worker bee than queen bee.

An officer's wife learned early to tune in to the fine nuances of base politics. It was how you furthered your husband's career, kept your family intact and survived the long deployments with fellow military wives.

Finally, the discussion shifted to the topic Kristina was interested in—the altar flowers. Bending, Honey smoothed the pink blanket tucked around her daughter. "It's so inconvenient to have to travel out of town for floral arrangements."

Mrs. Davenport peered over the top of her purple reading glasses. "And considering the expense, it behooves us to find another solution."

Behooves? Mrs. Davenport reminded Kristina of the high-society clients with whom she'd worked as a part-time floral assistant during her college days in Richmond.

"The inn's garden won't be at its best till May." Honey's lips pursed. "What about your garden?"

Mrs. Davenport—the only one in casual, coastal Kiptohanock to wear purple tweed—lifted her chin. "Inglenook will also not be in full bloom until Garden Week in May."

Kristina had never actually known anyone whose house had a name.

Honey gave Mrs. Davenport a measured look. "Which, of course, works out perfectly for you."

Mrs. Davenport sniffed. "Inglenook has taken the Garden of the Year award for the last five years."

"Perhaps not this year." Honey batted her lashes. "It's probably best not to count your trophies before they bloom."

Kristina's mouth twitched. Garden divas. Got it. Stay out of the fray.

Mrs. Parks shook her head. "Ladies, let's get back to decorating the sanctuary of the *Lord* this Sunday."

As if taking on a life of its own, Kristina lifted her

hand. "What about an arrangement of *sasanqua camellia*? I have several bushes in bloom right now…" Horrified, she dropped her hand into her lap.

What on earth had possessed her to violate her personal policy of always flying under the radar? Rule one in navigating tricky social hierarchies—keep a low profile.

Evy leaned forward, her trademark heels planted on the pine floor. "I think that's a wonderful idea." Her ponytail swished as she angled toward Mrs. Davenport. "Don't you, Margaret?"

Mrs. Davenport stared at Kristina. "Do I know you?"

"Kristina Montgomery," she whispered and knotted her fingers in her lap. "My son, Gray, and I just moved to Kiptohanock."

Margaret Davenport's nose wrinkled. "A 'come here.'"

"Yes, ma'am." She was whispering again. "Weston Clark's sister."

"Which makes you related to the Duers." Mrs. Davenport pinched her lips together. "By marriage."

Already she'd fallen afoul of village politics. Blacklisted by association.

Honey bristled. "As is Evy."

Margaret Davenport, also known as the Kiptohanock grapevine, had a soft spot for the young librarian. Behind her fashionable horn-rimmed glasses, Evy's blue eyes sparkled.

Honey placed her palms on the armrests. "Which makes Evy my sister, too." She threw Mrs. Davenport a small smile. "By marriage."

Kristina should've asked Caroline, *her* sister by marriage, to draw Kiptohanock family trees to avoid any genealogical land mines.

Mrs. Davenport steepled her hands under her chin. "And where exactly do you live, Kristina Montgomery?"

"Outside town. Toward Locustville. I bought the Collier house."

Mrs. Davenport fluttered her hand. "Why didn't you say so in the first place? Eileen Collier's garden used to be a showplace." Her lip curled. "Before that no-good grandson of hers made her a recluse."

Canyon Collier, the no-good grandson? Despite how she appreciated him taking Gray to task regarding his attitude, unease needled Kristina. She needed to find out more about her attractive pilot neighbor. For Gray's sake, of course.

"The camellias sound lovely." The reverend's wife smiled. "What about the other Sundays of Lent leading to Easter, ladies?"

Kristina raised her hand again. "I have a garden border, mostly of fragrant old-fashioned violets."

Her eyes widened. Why couldn't she keep her mouth shut?

Yet she held her hands in front of herself to demonstrate. "We could place the violets in tiny frogs and group them around the base of the cross—"

"Purple violets would match the altar cloth." Mrs. Davenport uncoiled a smidgen. "And in my considerable experience, anyone who knows about a floral frog can't be all bad."

Not a ringing endorsement, but nevertheless…

Evy swiveled. "What's a frog?"

Mrs. Davenport motioned for Kristina to continue.

She took a breath. "Frogs are used in the bottom of vases and bowls to hold flowers upright in an arrangement. The frogs are usually made in a woven grid of wire spikes. Or a frog can be a round glass disk with holes. Popular in the 1940s, '50s and '60s." She flushed and fell silent.

Honey nodded. "Do you have any frogs we could use for the altar arrangement?"

Kristina didn't usually talk so much. She was far more

comfortable fading into the background. But flowers were a passion of hers. "I have my grandmother's collection of vintage frogs. Colored Depression glass."

"Depression glass?" Mrs. Davenport's eyes lit. "I love Depression glass." She waved a beringed hand. "In fact, I collect those myself."

The baby stirred in her car seat. Honey lifted Daisy and cuddled the child in her arms. "Sounds wonderful. Anything else blooming in your garden, Kristina?"

Kristina tilted her head, thinking out loud. "I have white and mauve Lenten roses. Some blooming daphne also."

Mrs. Davenport's steely gaze softened. "Lenten roses for the Good Friday service. What could be more appropriate?" A frown creased her brow. "But with my work at the library, I'm not sure I could get to your house and put together a bouquet this week."

Evy patted Mrs. Davenport's arm. "You're always saying how you're too busy because of social obligations. Why not put Kristina in charge of the altar flowers this Lenten season?"

The newlywed librarian winked at Kristina. "Anyone who knows the Latin name for a camellia probably can be trusted to arrange the flowers."

Agnes Parks straightened. "An excellent idea. After all, you promised to help me run the Easter egg hunt on the square, Margaret."

Mrs. Davenport's eyes narrowed as if she suspected an attempted coup. "That is true." She scowled at Kristina. "We have high standards here in Kiptohanock, Mrs. Montgomery."

Kristina gulped. "I'll do my best not to let you down, Mrs. Davenport."

Mrs. Davenport became brisk. "Then that item on today's agenda is settled." As she shuffled the pages in her lap, her eyes took on a gleam. "I have some ideas to make this year's pancake supper at the firehouse even more successful than last year. But it will require every hand on deck."

Filled with sudden self-doubt, Kristina wondered what she'd done. She wasn't a professional florist. Gray's sarcastic remarks about her competence, or lack thereof, replayed in her head. But she loved flowers and always felt most at ease in a garden.

Like Gray loved tinkering with airplanes? Was she making a mistake in trying to keep him from what he loved?

Kristina winced at the memory of the scorn in his voice. Was that how he viewed his mother? Fearful, unskilled and worst of all, boring?

Shell-shocked at Pax's sudden death, she'd retreated like a turtle into its protective cover. And she'd dragged Gray—against his will—in there with her.

Was it already too late? She'd been disturbed by the anger in Gray's voice. At his bitterness—toward her.

In trying too hard to keep Gray safe, had she already lost her son? Would Pax recognize the woman she'd become? Did she even like the woman she'd become?

She was tired of waking each morning to the all-consuming fear of what the new day could bring. She was drowning them both with her fears. She'd had such dreams before she married Pax.

Dreams she'd surrendered gladly as they pursued Pax's career. Dreams sublimated as the demands of being a wife and mother slowly eroded everything she used to be. Was it time to reach for those dreams again?

Could she recapture the joyful young woman Pax had fallen in love with? Didn't she owe it to Pax's memory, to Gray and to herself to try?

Perhaps she'd taken the first step out of her safety zone by joining the altar guild. As for Gray's job with Canyon Collier?

When the committee meeting adjourned, she detoured to the aquatic center work site before heading home. After a probing conversation with Sawyer Kole, she came to a decision.

She was determined to face her fears. And to take back her life.

Fortified with a takeout bag stuffed with Long Johns, Canyon steered the Jeep toward one of the side streets, which meandered from the town square like spokes on a wheel. Heading north on Seaside Road, he blew past the entrance to the Duer inn.

Past Pauline Crockett's—she'd been the first farmer to give his business a chance. An old friend of his grandmother's, and a true friend, word of mouth being everything in his business.

He also bypassed the causeway leading out to Weston Clark's renovated lighthouse. Bringing Kristina Montgomery to mind. And the inexplicable contempt she bore Canyon.

Maybe not so inexplicable. Perhaps Jade was right. The Collier reputation continued to precede him. Always would.

So when he pulled into the airfield and spotted Kristina and Gray on his doorstep, his gut sank. His hands throttled the wheel. If not Jade, then Kristina Montgomery might drive him to his knees. Or an early grave.

"Who's that?"

Parking beside the Subaru, Canyon sat in the Jeep with Jade for a moment. "Next-door neighbors."

Might as well get this over with. He didn't like how his heart thumped at the sight of the widow. Best to keep her at arm's length.

"She's pretty."

Not a news flash, but at Jade's wistful tone, he glanced at his niece. She could've benefited from someone like Kristina Montgomery in her life. Instead, she'd gotten Beech and Brandi.

And now him. No wonder the kid was screwed up. A recurring theme in the Collier family tree.

"Who's the goofy boy?"

Canyon shoved out of the Jeep. "His name's Grayson. He's not goofy. He's a nice kid. Good with motors." He grabbed Jade's duffel from the backseat.

She got out more slowly. "A geek, you mean."

Across the Jeep roof, he frowned at her. "Seeing as you're not exactly drowning with friends, it wouldn't hurt you to be nice. He could show you the ropes at school on Monday."

Her mouth flattened. "Who says I'm going to school on Monday?"

Canyon slung the strap of the bag over his shoulder. "Me and Child Protective Services, that's who."

She slammed the passenger door. "Like I'd hang out with a loser like him. Get real."

Her cynicism reminded Canyon of himself and Beech at that age. A defense mechanism. Or so he hoped.

Despite her name, he prayed she wasn't too jaded to be reached. That somehow Jade could yet be saved from the destructive path she was on. Although as he'd proven with her father, Canyon was the last one on earth who should mount a rescue.

He headed toward mother and son, waiting on the steps of his office and living quarters. Leaving Jade to follow or not. Because not only could you not force a horse to drink, it was futile to lead them to water unless they were thirsty.

But what did he know? He'd failed to save Beech from himself, and he'd probably fail Beech's daughter, too. He'd never been anyone's hero. Nor was he likely to be.

Gray threw up his hand. "Hey, Canyon."

His mother's lips thinned. At least Gray was pleased to see him.

"Mom said she wanted to talk to you."

That sounded ominous. Probably to announce she'd reported him to the FAA.

"And—" Gray smiled, looking beyond Canyon "—I wanted to say hello to Jade."

Kristina Montgomery shifted as she caught sight of his niece. He was aware of the impression Jade created. An impression he suspected she cultivated.

The skinny black jeans. Beneath the leather jacket, the too-tight shirt exposing her midriff. An eyebrow ring. The magenta-streaked hair. Oh, and the five studs piercing one ear.

Battle armor. He remembered it well. Donned to shock. Before the Guard had gotten hold of him.

Gray's mother stiffened as she got a good look. And something in his chest thundered. Was this the kind of reception Jade would receive from the rest of Kiptohanock?

He positioned himself between Jade and the Montgomerys. Kristina's gaze flitted to his. No one was more surprised by his sudden protectiveness than Canyon.

Gray extended his hand. "I'm Gray. You're Jade?"

Probably without realizing it, Jade inched closer to Canyon. An unfamiliar pang shot through his chest. He broadened his shoulders.

But Jade was nothing if not plucky on the uptake. "Only name I got. Try not to wear it out."

Gray smiled and let his hand drop, unoffended. "You were a little girl in the picture on Canyon's desk." His brown eyes shone with frank admiration. "You've grown up."

Kristina's eyes ping-ponged between her son and Jade. No way she'd allow her precious offspring within ten feet of somebody like Jade. Or him.

Disappointment dropped into his stomach like a lead weight. Though why he'd expected—hoped—for better from Kristina Montgomery, he didn't know. Fact was, he didn't know the widow at all.

Nobody was going to give Jade a chance to remake herself.

He ought to have realized that. Twenty years ago, he'd had to go off-Shore to receive his own fresh start. And for the first time, he regretted coming back to Kiptohanock. For Jade's sake.

Gray—bless him—wasn't put off by his mother's caution, nor repelled by Jade's tough-girl persona. He reached for the duffel slung over Canyon's shoulder. "Can I help? I'd love to tell Jade about school."

Jade stuck out her skinny hip. "I'm not going…" With one look at Canyon's expression, she rolled her eyes. "Fine." She marched up the steps to the office.

At the door, she pivoted on her boot heel. "Are you coming or not, Gray?"

Jade's green eyes glinted at Gray's mother. He gave his niece full credit for reading people. With a mother like Brandi, perhaps that was how she'd survived.

But Jade needed to realize she wasn't alone anymore. For better or worse—probably worse—she had Canyon. And he had her back.

Gray grinned. "Sure." He started after her until his mother took hold of his arm.

Canyon clenched his jaw. He wouldn't allow this woman to hurt Jade. Jade had already experienced more rejection in her short life than anyone should.

But Kristina Montgomery surprised him.

"I'm going to allow Gray to work for you after school, Mr. Collier."

Gray threw his arms around his mother. "Oh, Mom. Thank—"

"Hear me out." She held up her palm. "On one condition. I'd like to accept your offer of an airplane ride." She arched her eyebrow. "Before I agree to let Gray work here."

Canyon got a quivery feeling in his chest. There went his vow to avoid her. He fought against an irrational surge of gladness. "Sounds fair. I promise you won't regret it."

He swallowed. Real question—would he?

Chapter Four

Standing outside the airfield office with her son, Kristina hadn't expected the teenage girl in goth attire. And from the puppy-dog looks Gray sent Jade Collier, he'd never agree to remain on their side of the property line. Especially not if someone his age—and female—lived next door.

Her "good fences make good neighbors" philosophy took a nosedive. So she decided to try a new approach. Time to add a few more strategies to her solo-parenting tool kit. And according to Sawyer Kole, Canyon was not the brother with the criminal record.

She smiled at the Colliers. "Have either of you eaten lunch?"

Behind the heavy black eyeliner, some of the glare dimmed from the girl's remarkable green eyes. Despite the affected air of boredom, the child was as attractive as her father.

He didn't wear a wedding ring. As for the duffel bag? Maybe weekend custody. Or had he become a full-time single parent like her?

Canyon squinted. "Lunch?"

If Gray was determined to spend time at the airfield, Kristina needed to get to know Canyon and his daughter better.

Jade propped her hands on her skinny hips. "What're you offering?"

"Don't be rude, Jade." Canyon's gaze flickered toward Kristina. "We haven't had lunch, but we wouldn't want to impose."

"It's not an imposition. My invitation."

For the first time in a long while, Gray smiled at his mother. "That's a great idea, Mom. Real neighborly. Can we have pimento cheese?"

Canyon cleared his throat. "We don't want to put you to any trouble."

Gray winked at her. "Mom keeps pimento cheese in the refrigerator. Cuts those great triangle sandwiches, remember?" He laughed.

"No crusts?" Jade wrapped her arms around herself. "I saw that on TV once." She glanced at Canyon. "Unless you're too busy."

Kristina was touched by the expression on Canyon's face when he looked at his daughter. Hope mixed with a healthy dose of fear. A new emotion for the cocky pilot?

"I'm not too busy," he grunted.

From their awkward demeanor with each other, she wondered if Canyon and Jade had spent much time together. Pimento cheese sandwiches seemed an easy gesture to help them ease into their new situation.

She climbed the porch steps. "Let's get Jade settled and then we can meet at my house for lunch."

Canyon unlocked the door. "I didn't get much notice Jade was coming."

At his gesture, Kristina stepped inside. "I didn't realize you lived at the airfield, Mr. Collier."

He motioned the children inside, too. "It's Canyon."

Gray took Jade's duffel bag. "Canyon started living here after he sold his grandma's house to build his business."

Kristina's eyes darted to Canyon. His grandma's house, now her home?

She followed Gray down the front hall. Disconcerted

to discover her bookish child sporting an interest in girls. Another reminder Gray was growing up. Too soon, she'd be utterly alone. A shaft of the familiar fear clawed at her insides.

Through the open door to the right of the hall, she caught a quick glimpse of a desk overflowing with paperwork.

Canyon flushed. "Business is slow until planting season. I was figuring to catch up, but then the Wildlife Commission hired me to do a migratory bird count on the barrier islands and…" He shrugged.

The hall led to a tiny galley kitchen and an eat-in dining area overlooking the hangar and airstrip. The counter was spotless, and dishes sat drying on the drain board. Other than his desk, Canyon kept his living quarters neat and tidy.

Canyon moved past Jade. "I didn't have time to clean my bedroom or I would've put you there." He threw open an adjacent door. "So I inflated the mattress and—"

At Jade's quick inhalation, Kristina peeked over Gray's shoulder. An air mattress lay in front of a washer and dryer in the utility room.

Canyon shuffled his feet. "It's temporary, I promise."

The wrong thing to say. Jade stiffened, and if anything, the chip she wore appeared to grow.

His jaw tightened. "That's not what I meant, Jade. As soon as I clear out my stuff, we'll trade places."

Jade's gaze cut to the Barbie poster on the wall.

Kristina's eyes widened. "Barbie?"

Canyon stuffed his hands in his jeans pockets. "Jade likes Barbie."

"When I was six." However, her eyes glistened. "But thanks for remembering Canyon."

Jade called her father Canyon? And he hadn't seen Jade since she was six? What in the world?

Not Kristina's business. Still, he'd tried. And his effort tugged at Kristina's heart. "I have an idea."

Gray, Jade and Canyon angled.

"There's an extra bedroom Jade can use at our house until you get your living arrangements sorted."

"We couldn't—"

"I don't need—"

"Great idea, Mom." Gray hugged her.

The second time her son had voluntarily hugged her. Progress?

Canyon rubbed his hand on the back of his neck. "It's not that I don't appreciate the offer, but—"

"Do you have any food in the kitchen?" Kristina crossed her arms.

He shook his head.

She tapped her foot. "Extra sheets, a pillow and a blanket for the mattress?"

He bit his lip.

Men.

"Unless you'd rather not, Jade." Kristina dropped her arms. "We're strangers, after all."

Jade Collier seemed to be one of those slow-to-warm creatures. Perhaps Kristina shouldn't have said anything. Like with a gun-shy horse, maybe it was better not to rush things.

"We're still in the process of getting settled ourselves." She made an expansive gesture. "It's not much. But it's a bed and your own bathroom. If you want it."

Jade's startling eyes dropped to half-mast. "More than what I'm used to." She patted Canyon's arm. "Though I do appreciate the Barbie attempt." Her mouth curved. "Coming from a confirmed bachelor like yourself."

So that's how it was with Canyon Collier. Never married. She'd seen his type before with pilots. A woman in every port—airport, in his case.

But she liked how the girl cared about her dad's feelings. A good heart existed beneath the layers of face paint.

With chagrin, Canyon accepted her invite. And Kristina drove home alone to get a head start on lunch. Gray stayed behind to give Jade a tour of the aircraft.

As in plural. According to Gray, Canyon owned an AT 802—aka the yellow plane—a Cessna 172 and a helicopter.

Great, just great. As she drove the half mile via the road toward her bungalow, she suspected Gray had more on his mind than aircraft. Which was cute, in a first-crush sort of way.

But the very mature Jade was far too sophisticated in the ways of the world to give her late-bloomer son the time of day. Or at least that's what she hoped.

Exiting her car, Kristina sent a quick prayer heavenward that Jade would let Gray down easy. She actually prayed. For the first time in a while.

She hurried to prepare the guest room and to set out fresh towels. Grabbing a blank piece of paper from the printer tray, she scrounged Gray's desk for markers.

"Welcome to Kiptohanock, Jade," she wrote with a flourish of curling vines and flowers onto the border. She taped the sign to the bedroom door.

In the kitchen, she slathered pimiento cheese on slices of white bread. Slicing the crusts from the sandwiches, she cut the bread into triangles. And smirked.

At how predictable she'd become. Although, on second thought, maybe not such a good thing. Was she as boring as Gray believed?

Plating the sandwiches, she heard the sound of a car in the driveway. Then Gray's voice.

"The Cessna 172 is a workhorse..." The screen door squeaked as her son bounded into the kitchen. "The carburetor needs tweaking, but I think I can..." Jade followed.

Canyon's broad shoulders filled the doorway. Jade's gaze flitted from the vintage mint-tiled border above the countertop to the small bunch of purple crocuses on the farm table.

Gray pulled out a chair at the table. "Please take a seat, Jade."

Kristina's heart warmed as her son went all Southern gentleman. Jade gave Gray a suspicious look. As if she expected he'd yank the chair out from under her.

But scowling, she sat down. Mouth curved upward, Gray plopped into a chair opposite Jade. "Thanks, Mom. Looks great. As soon as Canyon and I have time, we're going to take apart the…" He returned to his aircraft monologue.

She'd never known her son to be so talkative. Her eyes met Canyon's.

He smiled. Which revealed two deep dimples bracketing his mouth. Her heart did a strange flip flop.

Part of Kristina resented her son's hero worship of Canyon Collier. An adoration with which he'd only gifted his father.

After lunch, Gray volunteered to wash the dishes, the sheer novelty of his offer nearly sending Kristina into cardiac arrest. And leaving Gray to his sudden burst of helpfulness, she took Jade to her room.

Canyon hauled the duffel bag upstairs. At the sign on the door, Jade's stance softened before she caught herself.

Kristina leaned against the door frame. "Will this work for you, Jade?"

Jade let her shoulders rise and fall in a studied show of indifference. "Yeah. Whatever."

Canyon sighed. "Jade…"

Kristina bit back a smile. "It's fine."

"Teenagers. God's little way of keeping us humble."

She laughed. "True."

He deposited the duffel bag on the braided rug by the bed. His eyes crinkled at the corners as he took a long, slow look at the room.

Kristina turned to go. "I'll leave you to unpack, Jade."

Canyon joined her on the landing. "Thank you, Kristina. This goes way beyond neighborly. I'll tackle our living situation at the airfield immediately. We won't impose on your hospitality for more than tonight."

"No rush. It'll be nice having another female around." She tilted her head. "I was always outnumbered with Gray and his father."

Canyon's face shadowed. "I'm sorry about what happened this morning. I shouldn't have said what I did about your relationship with Gray being in jeopardy." His gaze shot toward the guest room. "Like you said earlier, what does a guy like me know about parenting?"

She sensed his discouragement. "Parenting teenagers is tough. I'm in no position to judge." She had an inexplicable urge to comfort him. "You obviously care deeply about your daughter."

"Wait. You think Jade is my—" Confusion flickered across his features. "I thought Gray explained."

Her cheeks burned. Why was it always *open mouth, insert a prop plane* when it came to Canyon Collier?

She fluttered her hand. "You don't have to explain anything." And hastened downstairs.

He caught her in the living room. "Jade isn't my daughter. She's my niece."

Kristina did an about-face. "Oh."

Canyon's brow creased. "Jade is my brother's child. Beech is in prison."

The brother with the criminal record.

Canyon gazed out the picture window overlooking the garden. "Jade's mother is one narcotic violation away from joining him." He inhaled. "I guess I'm all Jade has left, poor kid."

Kristina realized despite the arrogant pilot bravado, Canyon Collier had a lot of insecurities. "How did you get involved in flying? The Guard?"

"Before the Guard, actually. Hap Wallace was an old friend of my grandmother's. He taught me everything I know about flying."

Kristina remembered the sign at the airfield. "The Wallace part of the business."

"Hap started the business a long time ago. He became a father figure." Canyon dropped his eyes. "The only father figure I ever knew. I had no idea he'd leave the place to me in his will. After my grandmother died, I finished my Coast Guard enlistment and came back."

Kristina understood about loss. Canyon had lost his grandmother and his mentor in a short space of time.

"I returned to face the misdeeds of the past. To disprove the Collier family reputation."

She tucked a strand of hair behind her ear. "I admire the kind of courage it takes to confront your fears. I wish I were more like that."

Canyon was at a loss to understand the draw he felt toward the widow. "It takes a great deal of courage to pull up stakes after your husband's death. To move across the country and start a new life."

Kristina's shoulders slumped. "We needed a new place to begin again. Without reminders of everything we'd lost. Without seeing Pax at every turn."

Her hand groped for the chain hanging underneath her blouse. An unconscious gesture. Was her husband's wedding ring on the end of the chain?

A habitual gesture, he suspected, for a woman who'd been unable to move beyond her grief.

Canyon's heart felt heavy in his chest. "The airfield spoiled that for you. I'm sorry."

She shook her head. Tendrils of silky blond hair framed

her face. "It's my issue, not yours. I'm learning to live with it." Her hand clenched around the hidden chain.

Perhaps she'd moved on physically. But emotionally? He knew better than most that you couldn't run far enough to outdistance your problems. Though he'd certainly tried when he joined the Coast Guard.

"You've helped me so much already, jumping in to cover my failures with Jade."

She took a deep breath. "I'm beginning to realize I have you and your airfield to thank for making this transition easier on my son."

"Gray's a special kid. He has a real gift for mechanical devices."

"Like father, like son." Her chin quivered. "Which is exactly what I'm most afraid of."

As for Canyon's greatest fear? Getting too close and getting hurt. Again.

He'd not seen this coming when he spotted the moving truck a month ago on one of his aerial forays.

The next day, the gangly boy had appeared. Always on the edge of the forest, watching him take off in the early morning. Returning when Canyon landed the plane again.

One day the boy ventured closer to the hangar. He'd offered to help Canyon secure the plane and stow his gear.

He'd thanked Gray but refused his offer. Disappointment etched itself across the boy's features. Flushing, his eyes had dropped to his shoes.

Belatedly, Canyon remembered his own awkward phase. But Gray returned the next day and the next.

The shy, soft-spoken offer to help made each time. Hope springing eternal in his dark eyes. Until at last, after Gray waged a gentle war of attrition, Canyon surrendered to the inevitable and let the boy help out around the place.

"I appreciate your willingness to spend time with my

son." Kristina's wistful voice drew Canyon into the present. "He's missed that since his father's death."

Canyon's eyes flicked toward her hand, pressed against her blouse. Her fingers massaged the chain at her throat. Something stirred inside him. To be loved like that…

He'd never been loved like that. But then, he'd never opened himself to be loved like that. To be loved required love in return. And despite the inherent risk in his line of work, love was the ultimate risk he wasn't willing to take.

"Your husband sounds like he was a great guy." He hunched his shoulders. "A great dad and husband."

Something he'd never aspired to be. Someone he wasn't capable of becoming. Not for the first time, the Collier family mantle hung heavy.

At the clink of dishes, she turned toward the sounds of running water in the kitchen. "Pax was wonderful." Her face fell. "But he had a love affair with flying machines. A love that eventually took his life two years ago."

Canyon straightened. "The air disaster in Thailand?"

"No." Her mouth thinned. "Afghanistan."

His lips parted. "I didn't realize…your husband was military?"

She nodded.

An image emerged in his mind, based on other airmen he'd known. Solid guys. Intelligent. Gutsy. The kind who chose to put themselves in harm's way when bullets were flying. Heroes.

His admiration for the dead man rose. As did his admiration for Kristina. "You're a military widow."

Military wives didn't get the appreciation they deserved for their behind-the-scenes service to their country.

Her eyes clouded. "Our numbers are growing due to recent global conflicts. It's a club no one wants to join."

She leaned over to straighten the already tidy coffee

table. As much as anything, maybe to give her hands something to do.

His heart lurched. "You were the one left to pick up the pieces. To somehow put your family together again without your husband."

Kristina's mouth trembled. "Sometimes in dealing with Gray I think it would've been better if I'd been the one to die." Her voice dropped to a whisper. "Paxton was so strong. So confident." She sank into an armchair.

He eased onto the sofa. "I don't believe it would've been better for you to die. Gray wouldn't think so, either. He's just in a difficult phase right now. I've been there."

She shook herself. "I can't believe I'm telling you this. We're practically strangers."

Canyon longed to touch her hand, to reassure her. But he was afraid. Of himself and the way Kristina Montgomery made him feel. "Your son's trying to move beyond childhood—who he's been—toward who he wants to become."

She ran her thumb over the small exposed portion of the chain. "Aren't we all?"

"True enough. But I also think you don't give yourself enough credit. You're stronger than you realize."

Her eyes lifted to meet his. "You're incredibly easy to talk to, Canyon."

Canyon's eyebrow arched. "Nobody's ever said that to me before."

She raised her chin. "Maybe what I've needed is an objective ear."

He scrubbed his hand over his mouth. Objective? His objectivity when it came to Kristina and her son was decreasing by the moment. Scaring him, like he'd gone into a free fall and lost control of the aircraft.

"Maybe Gray and I are both on the threshold of becoming who we want to be. Who we were always meant to be." She tensed. "If only I could get beyond the fear."

"I know a surefire way to jump-start the process." He rubbed his suddenly perspiring hands across the thighs of his jeans. "Are you ready to get a tiny glimpse of your husband's world?"

She laid her palms flat on the armrest of the chair and studied him. "Your world, too."

"Gives me a new perspective every time. Monday morning after the kids go to school, how about you take that trip with me into the sky?"

Her eyebrows rose almost to her hairline. "In your airplane?"

Canyon's lips curved. "Unless you can flap your arms fast enough, yeah."

She gave him a shaky laugh. "So soon?"

He leaned his elbows on his knees. "Talk is cheap, Kristina Montgomery. Where's your sense of adventure?"

She squared her shoulders. "Are you daring me to go?"

He cocked his head. "Consider it a leap of faith. Gaining a God-sized perspective on where you've been and where you want to go. And I'll throw in a free flying lesson."

Kristina's mouth fell open. "Flying lessons? How did we go from an aerial tour of the Eastern Shore to me taking control of an airplane?"

He rolled his tongue in his cheek. "And here I believed taking control would be your thing."

She sniffed. "You don't think I'll accept, do you?"

He pursed his lips. "I think you can do anything you set your mind to. Trouble is, getting you to believe that, too."

She extended her hand. "All right then. You've got a deal." She glanced toward the kitchen. "But I insist you let me use my accounting degree and get your books up-to-date."

His hand closed around hers. A tingle shot up his arm. "Fair enough." He squeezed her fingers before letting go. "0900 sharp."

Canyon's heart raced with a mixture of dread and excitement. So much for avoiding the Widow Montgomery. And he pondered just how much this flying lesson would cost him.

Chapter Five

On Saturday, Gray set off after breakfast to work at the airfield. Kristina expected Jade to be a late riser, but the teenager soon clomped downstairs in her black combat boots. And settled in a chair at the red kitchenette table.

Kristina leaned against the countertop, sipping from her second cup of coffee.

Over a plate of crispy bacon and steaming eggs, the teenager did a studied inventory of the kitchen. "You like old stuff."

Kristina nodded. "Old-fashioned, but I find something comforting about the tried and the true." She took another sip. "I guess I'm hopelessly outdated."

Jade's gaze roamed from the vintage embroidered tea towel draped over the drain board to the red-checked gingham curtains at the window. "Not outdated. Retro. And it's cool." Her kohl-rimmed eyes caught Kristina's before sliding away. "Like a real home should look."

Despite Jade's air of indifference, she was still such a child. Kristina's heart ached at the grim picture Canyon had painted of Jade's childhood.

She couldn't understand why she felt so drawn to Jade. But she'd spent a lot of time praying last night—the second time in twelve hours—for wisdom in dealing with the raw, gaping wounds in the girl's heart. Beneath the layers of makeup and metallic ear studs, Kristina sensed a genuine goodness in Jade. Disillusioned and guarded, yet someone badly in need of a second chance.

Not unlike Kristina herself.

The makeup and the clothing, she suspected, were a way to deflect anyone from getting too close. A mask for Jade's low self-esteem.

Jade pushed away from the table. "Thanks for breakfast." The chair scraped across the black checkerboard linoleum. "And for letting me spend my first night here." She carried her plate to the sink. "I'll wash the dishes. I owe you."

Kristina set her cup on the counter. "You don't owe me. Neighbors being neighborly is the Kiptohanock way."

Jade gave her a look out of the corner of her eyes. "For real? Like Mayberry?"

Kristina laughed. "Not quite, but something like that."

"I'm still going to wash the dishes for you."

Jade was eminently salvageable. Infinitely worth rescuing. But as prickly as a catfish. She'd need to move carefully with her.

She laid her hand on Jade's shoulder, squeezed and moved away before Jade could react. "You may be the best houseguest I've ever had. I'm not going to want you to ever leave."

A small smile curved Jade's mouth before she turned the smile into a frown.

"There's something else you could help me with today."

Jade turned on the faucet. "What's that?"

"I've got to cut some flowers in my yard."

Jade plugged the drain and squirted detergent under the spray of water. "Why?"

"For an altar arrangement at the worship service tomorrow."

Jade's jaw tightened. "I don't know anything about flowers." She scrubbed the plates.

"I could use your help. It's a two-person job, especially when it comes to transporting the vases."

"Whatever."

Taking that as near to an affirmation as she'd get, Kristina dried while Jade finished washing the dishes. "Go get your coat. It's cold outside."

Jade took the stairs two at a time and returned with her coat.

Retrieving a plastic bucket from underneath the sink, Kristina filled the bucket halfway with lukewarm water. She lifted the bucket out of the sink and set it between them.

After donning her own coat, she extracted a flat, open basket from the confines of a Hoosier-style cupboard. "Tools of the trade." She laid two orange-handled clippers inside the basket.

Jade heaved the bucket of water. "I'll carry this for you."

Kristina smiled. "Thank you, Jade. That's so considerate of you."

To illustrate how little she cared, Jade scowled.

Note to self—praise Jade more often for good work.

The basket on her arm, Kristina shoved open the door with her shoulder. Lugging the bucket, Jade sloshed into the backyard.

"Morning is the best time to cut flowers, when the stems are fully hydrated. In the heat of the day, the petals droop."

Jade shot a scoffing look at the overcast winter sky. "What heat?"

Kristina headed toward a bright spot of pink blooming amid a profusion of dark green leaves. Placing the basket on the ground, she motioned for Jade to set the bucket alongside.

The look on Jade's face was comical when Kristina handed her one of the clippers. "You want *me* to cut the flowers?"

Kristina took the other pair and opened the blades along

a stem line. "Look for a branch with multiple buds. One bud should show color and another just starting to open."

Jade reached for a higher branch. "Like this one?"

"Good eye." Kristina positioned her clippers. "Now slice at a forty-five-degree angle about an inch from the bottom. Where it joins the main stem line."

"I can't." Jade backed away. "I'll butcher the bush."

Flagging self-confidence. Kristina recognized the feeling all too well. And refused to be put off by Jade's thorny demeanor.

"Just try. No harm, no foul."

The teenager glared. "That sounds like something Canyon would say."

Kristina tilted her head. "Even if you mess up the first time, you'll do better the next. The flowers will grow back."

Jade made an elaborate shrug. "It's your bush. Don't blame me when I kill it."

They worked in silence. Cutting flowers was not the time to dilly-dally. It was important to immerse the cut stems immediately.

"Pruning the shrub is actually good for the long-term health of the plant."

Jade eyed Kristina. "How's that?"

"Master gardeners know that periodic cutting promotes future flowering. Like deadheading."

Jade snorted. "Sounds like a zombie heavy metal band."

"What do you mean?"

"Deadheading. You know, zombies." Jade tapped her forehead. "Dead. Heads."

Kristina laughed. "Did you make a joke, Jade Collier? A gardening joke?"

"Don't tell anyone." Jade batted her long dark lashes. "I have a reputation to maintain."

Kristina wanted to tell her she didn't need so much mascara on those lovely eyes of hers, but instead she deposited her clippers in the basket. "I think we have enough for the arrangement."

Jade took charge of the flower-laden bucket. "Are you a master gardener, Kristina?"

She held the door as Jade trudged inside. "No, I just like flowers. Put the bucket on the table, please."

Kristina put away the basket and laid several sharp cutting knives on the farm table. "Can I hand you the vases?"

Stretching, she removed several vases from the top shelf of the cupboard. She passed them one at a time to Jade and then carried a third one to the table.

With her finger, Jade traced the ivy vine across the front of one of the crackled, black-footed vases. "These look old."

"My mother's."

The girl sighed. "Canyon says this used to be his grandmother's house before she died. He and Beech grew up here."

Kristina frowned. "I didn't realize it was a family home when I bought it."

Which was crazy. Of course it had been some family's home. She just hadn't thought about it being *Canyon's* family home.

It made her pulse race to think of him here. Which was ridiculous. But it was strange thinking of a younger Canyon living here.

Kristina wondered which bedroom had been his. Maybe—based on his wistful reaction yesterday—the guest room where she'd placed Jade.

His feet might've dangled underneath this very farmhouse table—that and the cupboard she'd purchased with the property.

Kristina pulled out a chair and sat across from Jade. "And if I hadn't bought it, this would be your home. I'm sorry."

"I'm not sorry." Jade placed her palms on the scarred

wooden surface. "If you hadn't bought it, I wouldn't have ever met you." Her eyes cut quickly to Kristina's and just as quickly darted away.

But not quickly enough that Kristina failed to spot tears welling in Jade's misty-green eyes.

Jade lifted her chin. "Canyon needed the money to get the Cessna. You have to invest in a business if you want it to succeed. Update and diversify."

The girl had apparently listened more intently to Gray yesterday than Kristina had supposed.

Kristina cocked her head. "Aren't you the budding entrepreneur?"

Jade smirked. "Did you just make a joke, Kristina? A gardening joke?"

"Don't tell anyone." Her lips quirked. "I have a reputation to maintain."

Jade laughed.

Pulling one branch out of the water, Kristina showed Jade how to split the ends of the stalk. "It's called preparing the stem, so it can absorb more water."

"How'd you learn about this stuff?"

Kristina removed the lower leaves from the branch. "A part-time job at a florist shop when I was in college."

She handed another stem to Jade. "Leave the pair of leaves closest to the blossom. Remove the rest. They foster bacterial growth when underwater."

Kristina placed small pin-holder frogs in the bottoms of the vases. After positioning a few stems, she left a skeptical Jade to finish filling the vase and start on the other two.

As she poured a bottle of lemon-lime soda into a pitcher, Jade crinkled her nose. "Is that for us to drink?"

"For the flowers to drink."

Mixing one part soda to three parts water, Kristina added a few drops of bleach. She returned to the table with the pitcher and surveyed Jade's handiwork.

"You've got the touch."

Jade stiffened, unsure if she was being mocked.

Kristina filled the vases three-quarters full with the liquid mixture. "The floral designer touch. These look great."

Prompting another scowl. "Really?"

"Couldn't have done better myself."

Jade's shoulders relaxed a tad. "What now?"

"We need to transport these to the church." She hurried to clear their workspace. "Tomorrow's the first Sunday in Lent."

Kristina nestled the vases side by side in a plastic tub so they wouldn't overturn on the ride to Kiptohanock.

With Jade in the passenger seat holding the tub in her arms, they reached the village without mishap. Kristina parked outside the church as the sun peeked from behind a cloud.

Inside, Jade's steps faltered. Her eyes cut from one side of the church to the other. The wooden pews. The stained-glass depiction of Jesus above the baptistry behind the pulpit. And finally rested on the gleaming altar cross.

"I've never been inside a church before," she whispered.

And suddenly Kristina was glad her upbringing had included the church in Richmond where she'd met and married Pax. A heritage she'd taken for granted.

She recalled other sanctuaries, too, scattered across a half dozen bases, where she'd found comfort during Pax's long deployments. Where she'd taught Gray about faith.

Kristina gulped past the rising emotion, remembering one final time in her Richmond home church at the memorial service for Pax.

Looking back on her grief, she wasn't sure how she would've survived without her parents' steadfast support and the gentle, uplifting comfort of her church family.

She was ashamed at how she'd turned away from her faith. And at the example she'd set for Gray these last two years. Hers had been a surface faith since Pax died. She'd been so hung up on the why and the unfairness of his death.

In the stillness of the Eastern Shore sanctuary, for the first time in a long while, she experienced a yearning to make her faith real again. One look at the teenage girl's face and Kristina knew Jade felt something, too.

Something powerful and lovely in this place. A holy place, a sacred place. Because of the One who dwelled here in the midst of His people.

Her footfalls hushed on the carpet, Jade carried the tub of flowers to the altar. "What's Lent, Kristina?"

She explained the significance of the weeks leading up to Easter, another term that required an explanation. Jade listened as Kristina placed the two taller vases on either side of the cross. "Let's put the oval one in front."

Jade stepped away to admire the effect. "Why three?"

"Florists always work with three." She touched the base of the brass cross. "Seems especially appropriate here. Father, Son and Holy Spirit."

Jade paused beside a stained-glass window picturing a bright light shining upon Jesus in a garden. "Canyon's grandma sent me a storybook Bible when I was little." Her mouth drooped. "But I lost it. We moved a lot."

"Life started in a garden." Kristina gathered the empty tub. "God's the ultimate master gardener." She stopped at the end of the pew.

Sunshine glimmered specks of purple, green and gold on Jade's upturned face. "And does He cut and prune to make more blooms on His plants, too, Kristina?"

Moving toward the front pew, Kristina halted midstride. Her eyes cut from the window to the flowers. Memories of Pax filled her senses. "You're right, Jade. I think He must."

Kristina blinked away tears.

* * *

Canyon was fluffing a pillow when he caught sight of Kristina's car. She parked next to his Jeep outside his office.

Gray rubbed his hands in anticipation. "They're here."

Canyon watched the long-legged, jeans-clad Kristina unfold from the car. Her blond hair held back from her face in a messy ponytail, she called to Jade, who removed a white takeout bag from the backseat. Kristina balanced a tray of drinks in her arms.

He didn't like the way his heart clicked in response to the sight of Gray's mother. The Widow Montgomery, he reminded himself. The very widowed Montgomery. Off-limits. Only turbulent storm winds ahead with that one.

"Uncle Canyon?" Jade called from the kitchen. "We brought lunch."

Gray loped from the bedroom down the hall. "Hooray."

Canyon followed more slowly, giving his heart time to return to its normal steady clip. Though not a real possibility any time he got within six feet of Kristina.

He stuttered to a stop as Kristina set out paper plates on the table. Her eyes tremulous and wide, she smiled. A shy, uncertain-of-its-welcome smile.

And Canyon gave up resisting as a lost cause.

She brushed a stray tendril of hair off her cheek. "Hi."

Canyon cleared his throat. "Hey."

Her slim hands removed burgers and cartons of fries from the bag. "We figured you guys probably hadn't taken time for lunch."

Jade chewed on a French fry. "So we stopped for you." She munched and swallowed. "Tammy and Johnny's."

Kristina shrugged out of her blue pea coat. "I wasn't sure we'd find you inside the house."

Canyon sat down before his knees gave out on him.

Gray seized one of the burger-laden plates. "We've been busy." He nudged Canyon with his elbow. "Real busy."

His eyes gleamed like a kid who longed to spill Christmas secrets.

Canyon toyed with a French fry. "You've got this teenager-parenting thing down, don't you, Kristina?"

"What do you mean?"

Canyon laughed. "As long as you feed them, they stay relatively manageable."

Her mouth curved. He lost himself for a second in her china-blue eyes. Dazed, he stuffed the French fry in his mouth.

"The care and feeding of adolescents." She sank into the chair opposite him. "Sounds like a self-help book."

He swallowed. "A self-help book I need to read. You're the expert at this single-parenting thing. I should take notes."

She glanced over to Gray, giving Jade an elaborate explanation of the intricacies of high school block scheduling. "On-the-job training."

Kristina traced the condensation on the plastic cup. "I hope you don't mind, but after I dropped the flower arrangement off at church, I took Jade to Walmart. She'll need school supplies for Monday."

"I didn't think about that."

Kristina must think he was the worst parent ever.

"Thanks." He reached in his pocket. "I need to reimburse you. And for the food, too."

She waved her hand, a graceful gesture. "Next time your treat. Did you enroll her yet?" Reaching across the table, she touched his arm.

Electric fire sizzled his nerve endings. Just as quickly she retracted her hand. Had she felt the chemistry, too? Or was this attraction only him?

She clutched the chain around her neck. For once it hung outside her plum-colored sweater. And he realized it wasn't her husband's wedding ring that dangled.

Worse. His stomach dropped. She wore her dead husband's dog tags.

Sensing his scrutiny, she let go of the necklace and flushed. "Th-there's paperwork to complete. I had to do the same thing with Gray a few weeks ago. Otherwise, the first day is such an ordeal."

A custodial parent only twenty-four hours, and already he was failing Jade dismally. "But with tomorrow being Sunday…"

"No problem." Gray slurped his milk shake. "The school principal attends our church. I'm sure Mrs. Savage could bring the papers with her tomorrow and expedite the process."

Jade's eyebrow, the pierced one, rose. "Expedite?"

Gray buried his face in the cup.

Her quota of niceness depleted for the day? Canyon grimaced. A person could get whiplash from these adolescent mood swings.

Canyon shot Jade a warning glance. "I wouldn't want to bother Mrs. Savage when she's off duty."

Jade snickered.

Heat rode above his collar. "I mean when she's not at work."

Kristina smiled. "You can take the man out of the military, but you can't take the military out of the man."

She folded the paper napkin. "Mrs. Savage wouldn't mind. I'll call her. Neighbors being—"

"Neighborly?"

He wasn't sure the rest of Kiptohanock would feel that way about him and Jade. Once the principal discovered the new student was a Collier, she probably wouldn't be as accommodating.

Savage was an old Shore name. And seasiders had long memories. But then again, so did he.

Jade twirled the straw in her drink. "Kristina says the

overnight temperature inside the church will be perfect. The blooms will be fully open by morning."

Kristina sat with her elbow propped on the table, her chin nestled in her hand. A fond smile on her face, she listened to Jade describe the arrangement they'd put together.

"Don't you want to see it, Uncle Canyon?"

His attention snapped from his contemplation of Kristina to his niece.

"Don't you want to see what I did?"

Green eyes bored into his. He was forcibly reminded of the last time he'd seen Jade ten years ago. The little six-year-old—with eyes too enormous for her face—waving as he rode away from the tenement she lived in with her mother.

"Sure, we'll go," he said, his voice gruff.

Gray punched the air and whooped. Jade's eyes glistened. Kristina stood to clear the table.

Canyon rose, too. He might be a reprobate, but Hap had trained him to be a gentleman.

Kristina pushed her chair under the table. "Time to go, Gray." She deposited the plates into the trash bin.

"We can't go yet, Mom. Canyon has a surprise for Jade."

Canyon shook his head. "If your mother needs you to go…"

Jade bounced up, abandoning nonchalance. "A surprise? For me? Where?"

Gray grinned. "This way."

Jade's eyes ping-ponged from Gray to Canyon. "In the office?"

"Come see," Gray called, already in the hallway. Needing no further encouragement, Jade headed out.

Canyon waited for Kristina. "Ladies first."

Her beautiful eyes clouded, Kristina ducked her head as she passed him on the threshold.

Gray stood poised at the closed door. "Ready, Canyon?"

He nodded, and with a flourish Gray threw open the door.

With the timidity of a child who'd long ago decided most surprises were bad, Jade stepped inside. Temples pounding, Canyon hung back.

Her eyes had gone wide. Her lips parted, but no sound emerged.

Canyon crossed his arms. This had been a bad idea. What did a guy like him know about what pleased a teenage girl?

Jade moved beside the bed and fingered the green-and-white tree of life quilt.

"Do you like it? Green like your eyes." Gray practically bobbed in his sneakers. "Canyon had his grandma's stuff stored in the loft. We moved out his office furniture, set up the bed—"

"I didn't know your favorite colors." Canyon propped against the wall. "We can change the bedspread. Buy a new one. Paint the walls whatever you want."

Jade wouldn't look at him. He scrubbed his hand across the back of his neck. This had been a bad idea.

Her gaze remained locked on the quilt. "I love it. Was this one of your grandmother's quilts?"

Canyon's pulse quieted. "Eileen Collier was your great-grandmother. These things were hers." He motioned from the walnut vanity dresser to the inlaid shell jewelry box. "But if you don't like hand-me-downs…"

Jade shook her head so hard the magenta feather strung in her hair fluttered. "I like old things." She sank onto the mattress. "Lived-with, loved-in stuff."

She ran her hand over the tree pattern appliquéd onto the solid white covering. "I love family things. This is perfect, Uncle Canyon."

A lump lodged in his throat.

Kristina squeezed his arm. "Well done," she whispered.

At last, maybe he'd done one thing right. "First hurdle in single parenting passed?"

"With flying colors."

He sighed, savoring one small victory. Tomorrow would bring further obstacles. Who was he kidding? He'd probably fall flat on his face within the hour.

"Maybe single parents like us ought to team up?"

He turned so quickly at her pensive words, he felt a crick in his neck. "What?"

She bit her lip. "Combine skill sets. Conserve our resources. Divide and conquer."

His heart hammered. What was she suggesting?

"The care and feeding of adolescents, remember? We can help each other." She blushed. "You're helping me with my fear of flying. I can help you with your fear of parenting."

When he didn't say anything—he wasn't sure what he ought to say—she fiddled with the hem of her sweater. "Gray told me most of your dusting takes place in the early morning. I could do morning carpool, and you could do afternoon pickup."

"Share the load?"

"Exactly. Besides, Gray is hungry for a positive male influence in his life."

Canyon wasn't sure he qualified for that title. On the other hand, did he need a reason to justify wanting to spend more time with the intriguing widow? If he did, she'd offered him one on a silver platter.

Only a fool would refuse such an opportunity. And no matter what else his mother had done, she'd not raised him to be a fool. Beech, yes. Him, not so much.

"That sounds like an offer I can't afford to refuse."

A smile touched her lips and reached her eyes. She started to extend her hand, perhaps reconsidered, and dropped it. After that last sizzling contact at the table, Canyon wasn't sure whether he should feel sorry or relieved.

"Friends?"

Canyon tucked his hands into his folded arms. "Friends."

For his part, could he keep their relationship friends only? And with dismay, he reflected that his mother might have raised more than one foolish son after all.

Chapter Six

Shutting off the buzzing alarm clock on Sunday morning, Canyon reasoned if Jade proved reluctant to get out of bed—didn't kids need their sleep?—he wouldn't push the church thing.

But when his bare feet hit the cold wooden floor, his nose alerted him to the aroma of eggs. Lumbering down the hall, he discovered Jade stirring eggs in a skillet.

With an uncertain look, she glanced at him. "I made you some coffee."

His gaze shot to the percolating coffeemaker. "You didn't have to—" He cleared his raspy voice and tried again. "I'm used to just cereal…"

Spatula in hand, she frowned. "I didn't think about you not liking eggs."

For warmth, Canyon tucked his hands in the armpits of his T-shirt. "I like eggs. Where did you learn to cook eggs?"

"I watched Kristina yesterday." Jade shoveled three-quarters of the eggs onto his grandma's Corelle plate. "We need a good breakfast before church."

He jolted as a piece of bread popped from the toaster.

She snickered. "Nervous much, Uncle Canyon?"

He poured a cup of coffee and sat down at the table to nurse it.

She set the plate of steaming scrambled eggs in front of

him. "Real question is—are you nervous because I mentioned Kristina or because I mentioned church?"

He wrapped his hands around the mug and ignored her.

She laughed. "No comment, huh?"

He shoveled a forkful of eggs into his mouth. "I'm eating."

"I saw your reaction when she touched your hand yesterday."

Canyon darted a glance at Jade, chewed and swallowed. This one didn't miss much. Good to know. Best to keep that in mind for future reference.

"I don't own a suit or tie."

Sitting across from him, she gave him an amused smile. "Gray says that church is casual. You have a pair of khakis and a button-down shirt in your closet." She fluttered her lashes. "I checked."

Of course she had. He grimaced. He hadn't darkened the Kiptohanock church since his grandmother's funeral.

He wondered if he'd be welcome. Kristina seemed to think so. He wasn't so sure.

Jade didn't seem worried. She hustled him through breakfast and started to clean the kitchen.

He took the dishcloth out of her hand. "You don't have to wait on me, Jade. It's my job to take care of you."

Jade's lips—an interesting eggplant color today—tightened at the word *job*.

She crossed her arms over her sweater. The color of the sweater and the lipstick coordinated with the magenta streak in her hair. And she'd accessorized with an amethyst stud in one earlobe.

Jade's version of church appropriate. At least the sweater covered her midriff.

"How about we take care of each other, Canyon? Share the housekeeping?"

Miss Independent. He couldn't fault her. He was the same way. Maybe one of the better Collier traits.

"Deal."

When he finished the quick kitchen cleanup, he discovered the aforementioned trousers and shirt lying across his bed.

"Don't make us late, Canyon," she yelled.

Five minutes later, she hurried him out the door. "We don't want to be those people who arrive after the service has started. Everyone turns around and stares. Gray warned me that latecomers have to sit at the front."

Canyon let the engine idle. "No, we definitely don't want to be those people."

He drove to Kiptohanock. Parking, he took a deep breath as they got out of the Jeep.

Jade clutched him as they walked toward the church. "Maybe this wasn't a good idea, Canyon. We can go home if you want."

But Gray waited for them on the church steps. And before Canyon could hit the proverbial brakes, they were escorted into the sanctuary. Immediately, his internal radar located Kristina as she chatted in the aisle with her sister-in-law, Caroline.

Jade heaved a sigh as Gray herded them toward—yes—the front. And Gray believed it to be his mission to introduce them to every churchgoer.

Most of whom Canyon already had a nodding acquaintance with from his youth. Everyone was surprisingly cordial. Not the condemnation he'd feared.

But Kristina's brother, Weston, gave him a wary look. "I checked your service record, Collier. I've still got friends in high Coastie places. Heard about your commendation."

Canyon's gut twisted. "I never asked for that." His gaze cut left, then right, hoping no one else had heard.

"You earned it. Otherwise I wouldn't let you within ten

feet of my sister and nephew." He shook Canyon's hand. Hard. "But don't think for a moment I won't be standing watch."

Canyon got the message. Hurt his family and Canyon would deal with Weston Clark.

Which Canyon totally understood. He took a long look at the teenage boys clustering around newcomer Jade. He'd feel the same way about her.

Then a friendlier face appeared. Sawyer and his wife, Honey. Canyon made appropriate noises of admiration over their baby, Daisy, who really was cute. But kids, on the whole, scared Canyon. Kristina joined them.

Which produced a terror of a different kind in Canyon's rapidly beating heart.

Seth Duer, the patriarch of the Duer clan, eyed him for a moment before shaking his hand. "I knew your mother, Amber, a long time ago. Never had the privilege of meeting your dad."

Canyon shrugged. "You and me both."

Kristina gave him a startled look.

He was so not the poster child for family of the year. "Amber wasn't one to stick around any place too long. A real wild child."

The older man's bristly mustache curved. "I 'spect that's the truth of it. Even as a girl, your mother was always the free spirit."

Canyon rolled his tongue in his cheek. "She still is. Or last I heard. A rolling stone."

Earning an appreciative chuckle from the aging waterman. "I hear you, son." Seth clamped a firm hand on Canyon's shoulder. "May I call you son?"

Canyon's throat thickened. "First time for everything, huh?" He reddened under Kristina's searching gaze.

Seth's blue-green eyes studied him. "Sawyer tells me you're good people. And if Sawyer says you're okay, you're okay. We should get together at the Sandpiper over Long Johns soon."

Canyon recognized he'd just been given a community seal of approval. "I'd like that, Mr. Duer." He gulped. "A lot."

"Good." Seth squeezed Canyon's shoulder and dropped his hand. "I'll look forward to it."

When the organ prelude began, he found himself and Jade seated between Kristina and Gray. It hadn't escaped Canyon's notice how Gray's features lit whenever Jade got within five feet of him. Canyon hadn't forgotten what it felt like to be a gawky fifteen-year-old boy. Around Gray's mother, he knew the feeling all too well.

He vaguely recognized the opening song and shared a hymnal with Kristina.

O God, our help in ages past, our hope for years to come. Our shelter from the stormy blast and our eternal home.

Thereafter, it was a matter of standing or sitting as the bulletin indicated.

From the pulpit, Reverend Parks read about soaring on wings like an eagle. Soaring was something Canyon understood. Soaring in life—a yet unrealized goal.

The scriptural discourse provided an unexpected solace. The reverend was also a contemporary of Canyon's erstwhile mother. She'd been the first in a long line of Colliers to discredit the family name. Like mother, like sons.

Like Jade? His mouth tightened. Not if he had anything to say about it.

Afterward, because it was a fourth-Sunday-of-the-month tradition, Long Johns and hot coffee were served in the fellowship hall. He snagged a powdered doughnut off a serving tray. This time of year, there were few tourists, only the faithful year-round Kiptohanock residents.

Somehow Canyon found himself surrounded by a group

of men. Sawyer led the effort in recruiting him to help with the volunteer fire department's pancake supper in a few weeks.

He elbowed Sawyer. "Thanks a lot, my friend." But he acknowledged the effort for what it was—a way for him to prove himself among the Kiptohanock men.

Unrepentant, Sawyer grinned. "That's what friends are for. Getting you plugged into the community." The ex-Coastie smirked. "Kicking or screaming."

He bit into the Long John. This whole church thing hadn't been as bad as he'd feared. Either no one remembered what Beech had done or chose not to blame him and Jade for Beech's crimes.

Kristina received many compliments on the altar arrangement, a recognition she duly shared with Jade, who blushed as vividly as her sweater at the praise of the women. In her eyes Canyon caught a flicker of pride.

And perhaps the partial melting of the glacier that was Jade Collier.

Kristina gave Jade a one-armed hug. "Next Saturday? Same time, same job?"

"Really?"

Jade didn't pull away. A first. He gave full kudos to Kristina and her way with those of the teenage species.

Kristina smiled. "You're the best floral assistant I've got."

Jade's tinted lips pursed. "I'm the only floral assistant you've got."

"Exactly." Kristina tapped her chin with her forefinger as if thinking out loud. "About that border of violets…"

As they moved away to make plans, the high school principal cornered him in the annex. He spent the next twenty minutes filling out Jade's registration papers.

"I hope your niece will have a successful school year, Mr. Collier."

Mrs. Savage had been a media specialist when he and Beech shadowed the hallowed halls of learning. Like Seth Duer and the reverend, she was also a contemporary of his mother's.

He flushed. To the best of his knowledge, Beech hadn't defaced any library property. At least, Canyon prayed not.

Who'd have thought? Him, Canyon Collier. Praying. Between Jade and the church thing, Canyon would be on a first-name basis with the Creator before long.

"Believe me, Mrs. Savage, no one hopes that more than me."

Should he address the elephant in the room? Mrs. Savage settled the issue for him.

"The past is the past, and I want you to know, Mr. Collier, we're here to help your niece make a smooth transition. I'll place Jade in the sophomore class, pending receipt of her official transcripts."

He shuffled his feet. "I appreciate that, Mrs. Savage."

She eyed him over pink-framed reading glasses. "The sins of the father won't be charged to Jade's account on my watch. But having said that, I sincerely hope Jade will make good use of this opportunity."

"I'll make sure she does. Not many of us get a chance to start over again."

Mrs. Savage removed the glasses from the bridge of her nose and let them dangle from the beaded chain around her neck. "You've done well for yourself, Mr. Collier. You needed a course correction, but once Hap Wallace put you on the right path, you've sailed clear and true with the wind."

"Fair winds and following seas, ma'am."

She smiled. "I'll introduce myself to our high school's newest student."

As she headed toward his niece, Canyon prayed he and Jade would prove worthy of her trust.

Later, he invited the Montgomerys to join them for lunch. "My treat."

Kristina bit her lip. "You don't have to—"

"I want to." He locked gazes with Kristina. "How about the Sage Diner?"

She followed his Jeep to the restaurant on Highway 13. Since it was a popular spot to eat lunch, they had to wait for a table. Gray and Jade amused themselves by reading the local ads posted on the community board.

"You're not going to chicken out on me, are you, Kristina? We still have an appointment tomorrow morning, right?"

She kept her focus glued on the laminated menu. "I'll pick up Jade about seven fifteen."

"That's not the appointment I meant." He leaned against the chair railing in the lobby. "But I appreciate how you've taken Jade under your wing."

Kristina's gaze rose above the edge of the menu. "Like you've taken Gray under yours." Her lips quirked. "Literally."

He scrubbed the back of his neck with his hand. "I have the feeling Jade will go with less duress if you're the one to drop her off."

"Jade is going to be fine.

"I wish I had your faith."

She blinked. "My faith?"

"Faith has always come hard for me." He blew out a slow breath. "But maybe in the long run, when it's hardest is when faith means the most."

Kristina swallowed. "Something I'm still learning. Though I think you may be right."

"Another first."

Her expression eased. "A first that you're right? Or a first that I agree with you?"

"Take your pick."

When she smiled, he thought his heart might go into overdrive. He strove for a nonchalance he didn't feel. *Cool your jets, man.* He cared way more about the widow than he ought to.

After lunch, he couldn't get out of there fast enough, but Jade wanted to linger over dessert. So Kristina offered to bring her home.

He was already regretting his offer to take Kristina in his airplane. But it was too late to back out now. And considering who he was, it was probably too late for a lot of things.

On Monday morning, Kristina drove the kids to school. Jade huddled in the backseat, sullen to the point of silence. Gray overcompensated by chattering nonstop.

Gray was nervous for Jade. A nervousness Kristina shared. The teenagers lurched out of the car and plodded toward the entrance. Jade looked like a prisoner headed for the firing squad.

Kristina said yet another prayer for Jade. Returning home, she made a few phone calls regarding employment, emailed a few résumés.

Rattling around her empty house, she couldn't help counting the minutes. And at 0900 sharp, she reported to the airfield.

Music blared from the loudspeaker attached to the corner of the hangar. An old song. The Big Band sound of World War II.

"A sentimental journey," a long-dead singer warbled. Was that what this was about for her? A journey to reconnect with Pax? Or a journey toward the rest of her life?

She hovered on the precipice of a new world. The sensation was both thrilling and terrifying. Her anxiety mounted.

Kristina scanned the hangar for signs of Canyon. Skirting a workbench, she followed a trail of oil rags to a truck.

A pair of legs in dark blue overalls poked out from beneath the undercarriage.

His rich baritone emanated from below. She smiled at Canyon's crooning about setting his heart at ease.

Fears momentarily forgotten, she crouched beside the dolly and thumped the truck with the flat of her hand. "Canyon?"

"Kris?" He sat up so fast he banged his head. "Ow!" He fell back.

The sound of her abbreviated name on his lips gave her a fluttery feeling. No one had ever called her that before. A new name for a new life?

She peered underneath the truck. "Are you okay?"

Using his legs, he propelled the dolly out into the open. Rubbing his forehead, he gave her a sheepish look. "I didn't hear you come in."

She motioned toward the speaker as the old song wound to its conclusion. "No wonder."

He flushed. "A favorite of my grandmother's."

She tilted her head. Grease streaked his cheekbone. "If the aerial application business doesn't work out, you can always find work as a backup singer."

He laughed. "Thanks. I think…" The flash of even white teeth almost blinded her.

Wow, he was handsome. Heart-stoppingly so. Good thing her heart lay in a coffin at Arlington or—

Or what? She stood so quickly, her head spun.

His face constricted as if he sensed more than her physical withdrawal. He rose and extracted a semiclean grease rag from the pocket of his overalls. He swiped at his brow.

She pointed at her own cheek and gestured. He nodded and scrubbed his face. More forcefully than the stain warranted.

His blue eyes glinted. "Did Jade do okay this morning?"

"So-so. We'll see what she has to say this afternoon."

He grimaced. "Of that, we can be certain. Jade isn't one to hold back."

"But the good news is you'll always know where you stand with a child like her."

The playlist had moved into a rendition of "We'll Meet Again." She caught a whiff of Canyon's aftershave, interlaced with a faint trace of oil. The woodsy aroma set her pulses thrumming.

She took a step backward, poised to flee. This was a bad idea. An insane idea.

What was she doing here? Pax... Her hand flitted upward.

Canyon's hand shot out and caught her arm. She stared at his hand on her jacket.

"Winds are favorable. The plane's on the tarmac. Fueled and ready to go. Are you ready to give it a try, Kris?"

She moistened her lips. No fair when he called her Kris. She could grow attached to the sound of it.

"Last chance to renege." He released her arm. "It's up to you."

She missed the pressure of his fingers against her sleeve. And if she didn't go with him this morning, she had an unsettling feeling she'd be missing more than just a bird's-eye view.

He stepped out of his coveralls and tossed them onto a workbench. "I liked that verse yesterday. Appropriate for a pilot like me."

She searched her memory. Isaiah 40. "Those who hope in the Lord will renew their strength. They will soar on wings like eagles; they will run and not grow weary, they will walk and not be faint."

"That's the one."

He left the hangar and moved toward the yellow fixed-wing aircraft on the runway. He threw her a smile over his shoulder. Her insides got that bottom-dropped-out feeling like she'd gone airborne.

"Come fly with me, Kristina."

"What if I fall?"

Canyon offered his hand. "But what if you soar? Don't you think it's time to find out?"

Her heart jackhammered in her chest. But she slipped her hand into his.

One way or the other. Ready or not. Time to take a leap of faith. Time to soar.

Chapter Seven

The landscape outside the yellow airplane blurred. Faster and faster, the wheels ate up the runway. In the cockpit, Canyon gave Kristina a thumbs-up and pulled back on the stick.

Her stomach dropped for real this time. The plane lifted off the ground, climbing higher and higher. She panicked at the sight of the huge sycamore at the edge of the forest on the far end of the airstrip. But Canyon expertly cleared the tree. And she found herself at a dizzying height above the receding airfield.

The plane banked, the wing dipping. She clutched the straps of the belt holding her in the seat.

"Kristina?" Above the ear-pulsing roar of the engine, his calming voice drifted through her headset. "Are you okay?"

She loosened her death grip and nodded.

He tapped his finger on the attachment mounted on the headphones. "Fix the boom closer to your mouth so we can talk to each other. Or, every man's dream, I'll talk, and you listen."

She adjusted the tiny microphone. "I assure you my vocal cords are fully functional."

He gave her a two-fingered salute. "Duly warned." He nudged his chin at the window. "There's your house."

Inching forward, she peered out the window. The tin-roofed bungalow gleamed in the early-morning light. "I can't believe you can see the garden from here."

A beat of silence. Her eyes flicked to him. His mouth compressed into a thin line.

"My grandmother's idea. This time of year, the white camellias stand out from the ground. In the summer, it'll be the white gardenias."

"I love white gardens. They glow, even in the dark."

Canyon checked a gauge on the instrument panel. "She planted them to be visible from the air. A beacon of sorts."

"How wonderful." Kristina smiled. "The first thing you see when you're headed home."

A muscle pulsed in his cheek. "Not meant for me. Before my time. For someone else. For someone lost."

She sensed something more to his story, something painful. But his reserve stopped her from asking further questions.

Heading toward the coastline, he drew her attention to the lighthouse on the Neck.

She clapped her hands. "Weston's house."

Canyon brought the plane low over the waves. Thirty feet above the water, she fought the urge to draw up her feet. The cocky pilot shot her a teasing glance.

She gritted her teeth. "Dusting the waves, Collier?"

Eyes gleaming, he pulled the plane to a higher altitude. Her stomach nosedived again before the plane leveled out.

He flew north, tracing the outline of the Atlantic coastline. Over the tidal marshlands. Skimming the barrier islands.

Near Assateague, Canyon gestured at a herd of small horses below.

Her breath hitched. She leaned for a closer look at the Chincoteague ponies, which swam across the open channel of a tidal estuary between the barrier island of Assateague and a deserted portion of maritime forest.

She smiled. "I'm looking forward to Pony Penning in July with Gray."

Canyon groaned. "Please, don't tell Jade about it. Or I'll get roped into taking her to see it, too." His lips quirked. "Roped…did you catch what I did there?"

She made a face. "What's wrong with Pony Penning? It's an important moneymaker for the Chincoteague Volunteer Fire Department."

"True." He veered lower, giving her a better look at the wild horses. "The saltwater cowboys drive them over to the mainland, where they auction them off to horse lovers. If they didn't cull the herd, the rest wouldn't be able to survive on the scrub available on the barrier island."

"So what's the problem?"

He shrugged. "Kind of a tourist thing. Locals stay away on purpose. Congested roads and restaurants. We lose our splendid isolation for the duration."

She wondered if that was how he regarded his hermit-like, pre-Jade existence. But visualizing him alone and isolated with only his airplanes filled her with dismay. Causing Kristina to feel oddly off-kilter.

"What would you suggest about Pony Penning Day then?"

He performed a 180 and headed south again. "Watch the swim on the local news. Read the book and visit Chincoteague the week after penning. Many of the horses are still corralled and accessible before being shipped off to their new owners."

"You've read the *Misty of Chincoteague* children's book?"

He snorted. "Every child on the Eastern Shore of Virginia, Maryland and Delaware has read the book. Required reading in elementary school."

"Gray likes to read. Probably too juvenile for him, but he's interested in local history."

Canyon shook his head. "It's your traffic jam. I'm just glad Jade is beyond the doll–princess–tea party stage."

Kristina smirked. "Right, 'cause the raging hormones–puberty–dating stage is so much easier."

"When you put it that way…"

The airplane bypassed the lighthouse again. Her heart lifted at the sight of her favorite fishing hamlet ahead. "Kiptohanock already feels like home."

"Guess that's why I came back. Why did you? Why not Richmond where you grew up?"

"I met and married Pax in Richmond. He didn't have any family left. With too many memories of him there, we needed a fresh start in a new place. Having Wes and his family nearby was a bonus I couldn't refuse."

Canyon buzzed the harbor before heading west toward the bay. "Family is important. I'm glad you decided to settle in Kiptohanock."

She glanced at him. "Are you?"

"I don't know how I would've managed Jade without you. And Gray's a big help at the airfield."

"Are Gray and Jade the only reason?" As soon as the words left her mouth, Kristina couldn't believe what she'd said.

Canyon's gaze cut to hers. "No, not just because of the kids."

Her pulse accelerated at the look in his eyes.

The airplane droned over fields and farms. Its shadow followed the railroad track, a silvery ribbon of steel dividing the peninsula.

"Ready for a little barnstorming?" Canyon's face shone. "This is why I love aerial application. Fast and low and furious."

Her lips twitched at his mischievous expression. "Bring it, Collier."

Canyon's answering grin set her heart clamoring. "Hang on, Kris."

The air rushed past as he guided the plane low across a fallow field. Thrusting the stick sharply toward his chest, he brought the nose of the plane over the trees. She gasped at the power lines ahead.

But just as quickly, he went under the lines. Up and over and under. Again and again. Field after field. Intricate and highly skilled maneuvers. With great finesse and concentration.

For the first time, she felt the thrill that had enraptured Pax and Canyon. She experienced the feathery freedom of the world falling away. And with it, all of its cares and entangling fetters. She exulted in the joy of the blue sky.

He smiled at her happiness. "I'd love to teach Gray to fly. It's his dream."

Kristina couldn't find fault with the condition of Canyon's aircraft or his flying skills. Gray could learn a lot from this pilot. As from the man himself?

She was more than impressed at the way he'd taken on the responsibility of his niece. Not many men would. But one thing she was learning about Canyon Collier?

He wasn't like most men. He wasn't like anyone she'd ever met. Which excited—and frightened—her.

"When the dream dies, the heart grows cold," she whispered.

He jerked, something strange in his expression. "W-what have you heard? Who told you about my grandmother?"

She frowned. "I know nothing about your grandmother. I was referring to what you said. About Gray and his dream."

"Oh, yeah. Gray."

She tilted her head. "What did you think I meant?"

He fiddled with the controls. "Does this mean I pass the test?" he asked, avoiding her question.

"I'm not sure I can afford flying lessons. I don't know how I'd repay you."

"Gray and I can work out an arrangement based on his help with aircraft maintenance. If that's okay with you."

Kristina had the undeniable conviction God had put Canyon into Gray's life for a reason. "I'd like that."

She was talking about Gray, right?

Kristina moistened her lips. "*Gray* would love that. Thank you. He seems to have clicked with you."

Canyon's eyebrow arched. "How about bonded? Sounds less girly."

She playfully punched his shoulder. "You know what I mean."

He batted his impossibly long lashes at her and her stomach knotted. There was nothing remotely girly about Canyon Collier.

"What about your flying lesson?" He took his hand off the stick. "Want to have a go landing the plane?"

She hadn't realized they were so close to home. They'd flown a big circle around the Shore.

Her hands fluttered. "No, I don't. Get your hand on the gearshift or whatever it's called before we crash."

Canyon placed his hand on the stick again. "Just teasing. Got everything under control."

She'd just bet he did.

"Except for parenting Jade. And for your help with her, I owe you. Far and above what you could ever owe me for teaching Gray to do something I already love."

Something he loved. A niggle of dissatisfaction spoiled some of her enjoyment of the day. She wished there was something—besides being Gray's mother—that she loved doing. Something to which she could give her heart.

Despite a worrisome doubt she might be setting in motion a course of events that could potentially end Gray's life—as it had his father's—she refused for once to give in to the fear. And with determination, she turned her attention to other things.

Like this too-handsome-to-be-real man beside her in the cockpit.

"What's a year in life of an aerial application specialist like?"

He gave her a lopsided smile. "Very good, Kris. You're learning the lingo."

He'd called her Kris again…

"Winter isn't too busy. With the Cessna, I can do aerial photography. I spend about six weeks doing surveys of the migratory waterfowl population for environmental groups. Come warmer temperatures—" he patted the console of the plane "—with this little baby, I spray mosquito larvae."

"Then growing season gets busy, I imagine."

"Pretreatment, and once the crops emerge, more work than I can handle."

"When do you use the helicopter?"

"There's the occasional scenic charter flight. I hope to grow that part of the business. I also volunteer to transport sick children on angel flights whenever I'm needed."

She was amazed at his skills. And his compassion. "You're very versatile."

"I have to be. Midsummer I head out west for summer fire season in the national parks for a few weeks."

She shuddered. "That sounds dangerous."

"Keeps me on my toes. It's fun."

"The things that amuse you, Canyon Collier…" She rolled her eyes. "You flyboys are like an alien species."

He winked. "Maybe in a few years, Gray will earn his pilot license and can become my partner."

She sighed. "I wish there were lessons for flying through the adolescent years. A heavy hand or a light one on the controls?"

"Like in life and in aviation, I suspect you have to know

your plane and be flexible to developing weather conditions. There's no teacher like experience."

"And," she huffed, "you probably need to pray a lot."

He eased a fraction off the throttle. "You said it."

"Which is why parents of teenagers should stick together."

He raised his palm. "Team Teen Parenting?"

She high-fived him. "Team Surviving Adolescence."

He lowered the landing gear. "Hang on. Some landings can be bumpier than others."

"Now you tell me." She clutched the seat belt. "Why do I get the feeling the easy part is taking off?"

"You wouldn't be wrong." He grinned as the plane descended. "It takes real skill to land this bird."

"That's what I was afraid you were going to say."

"Have some faith, Kris. This isn't my first rodeo."

Inhaling, she pressed her feet into the floorboard, as if by sheer willpower she could stop the plane. Which was about as useless as trying to hold on to her life with Pax. Or as effective as holding back time. She bit her lip.

The wheels touched down gently. But she focused on Canyon's steady hand at the controls. Capable and strong. He braked.

She shivered at the remembrance of his long, warm fingers on hers the other day. And she forgot to be afraid. Suddenly, she realized the plane had come to a complete standstill.

"A safe, smooth landing. Perfect, if I do say so myself." He removed his headset.

She made a face. "You don't lack for self-confidence, do you, Canyon?"

Reaching over, he helped her take off her headset. "I'm a man of my word."

"Would you be offended if I kiss the ground when I climb out of this sardine can?"

He unfastened his safety belt. "I'm not ashamed to admit I've kissed the ground after a few SARs with the Guard."

Canyon scrambled out onto the wing. "Let me help you." He dropped lightly to the airstrip.

Rounding the airplane, he wrenched open Kristina's door. "Thanks for flying with me today. And for agreeing to let Gray take lessons."

She grasped his hand as he helped her unfold from the cockpit. Crawling onto the wing, she hopped down. He didn't let go of her hand.

"Maybe one day you and I could catch a sunset in the clouds." He shuffled his feet. "Nothing beats an Eastern Shore sunset."

"I'd like that."

He looked at her then. A slow, crooked smile. "I'll look forward to it."

So would she. A giddiness, foreign to her usual equilibrium, seized hold of her at the idea of flying through a sky streaked with the glow of heaven.

Nothing beat sunset. Except maybe sunrise. With a certain aerial application specialist by her side. An unexpected recklessness overtook Kristina.

"Is your offer for flying lessons still open to me, too?"

His brow furrowed. "You're serious about wanting to learn to fly an airplane?"

Another step toward overcoming her fears and reclaiming her faith again. "I am."

He stared at her so long she was sure he was going to refuse. She felt foolish. Taking up a hobby like flying at her age—what was she thinking?

But that was the trouble. She didn't think much when she got close to Canyon. And like a numbed limb coming to life, the tingling pricks of returning sensation were a mixture of pain and reassurance.

"Never mind." She waved her hand. "You're probably too busy—"

"I'm not too busy. How about an hour first thing in the morning after you drop the kids off at school?"

"Uh…"

His eyes narrowed. "Unless you weren't serious about trying something new. Your call."

Canyon was giving her an out. A graceful exit. She replayed the yawning emptiness of her days while Gray was in school. She contemplated the weariness of always being alone.

Was Canyon as tired of being alone as she?

Her heart thumped inside her chest. "I want to learn to fly. Will you teach me, Canyon?"

"If that's what you want."

She gulped. "I do. But not too fast."

"You set the pace." His jaw tightened. "I'd never let anything happen to you."

She knew that about him. "Okay."

His shoulders relaxed a notch. "Same time tomorrow?"

"You've got yourself a date—I mean—"

"If you'd let yourself breathe, you might find you enjoy soaring above the trees."

Easier said than done, with him so near. More likely she'd find herself plummeting to the ground. What had she gotten herself into?

She didn't know what worried her more—operating an aircraft or spending every morning with the pilot at her side. On second thought, no contest. Spending time with Canyon promised to be far more hazardous.

At least to her heart.

Chapter Eight

According to Jade over tacos that night—the extent of Canyon's culinary prowess—her first day of school had gone moderately well.

She went to her classes. And created a buzz in the cafeteria with her metallic-studded attire.

Jade snickered. "The guidance counselor said I dressed postapocalyptic."

"Congratulations." He laughed. "Quite the impression you've made."

She waggled the stud piercing her eyebrow. "I try."

Jade didn't mind getting attention—bad or good. In that, he glimpsed her father, Beech. But if nothing else, she willingly returned for day two. And for a Collier, a win was a win.

He also had Kristina's first official flying lesson to look forward to. She arrived at the tarmac with coffee and a takeout bag from the Sandpiper Café.

Canyon leaned against the Cessna and adjusted the brim of his baseball cap. "Didn't get enough coffee before carpool?"

She held out the to-go mug. "It's for you."

"For—" He straightened. "Thanks. No one's ever…" He pried open the lid and took a sip.

Mainly to give himself something to do beside moon over

Gray's mother. He could get used to sharing his mornings with Kristina. Too used to Kristina Montgomery, period.

She didn't seem to notice his reticence. "What do I do first?"

He smirked. "Who's moving fast now?"

She tossed her hair in the glow of the morning sunshine. He caught a whiff of a beguiling floral scent.

"I'm eager to begin a new chapter."

He wasn't sure he believed her. "Baby steps." Though he was probably cautioning himself more than her.

She scoped out the runway. "Where's the yellow bird?"

He patted the wing of the larger white plane. "The Cessna is the best plane for a beginner. More straightforward. Less sensitive to the stick." He grinned. "But the AT's my favorite, too."

She smiled. "Fast and low and furious."

Over the next hour, he showed her how to do a ground inspection of the aircraft. She chatted about her childhood in Richmond. About life as a young mother on bases scattered across the United States. She revealed more of her married life than perhaps she realized.

A picture of Gray's father emerged in Canyon's mind. Of a pilot whose driving ambition and exuberant thirst for adventure often overshadowed his quiet, gentle-natured wife. Including any possible dreams she might have had for herself.

Eventually getting into the cockpit, he went over takeoff protocols and further safety checks. As she leaned closer to examine the controls on the instrument panel, he spotted the glint of the chain underneath the collar of her jacket.

He thought it interesting she'd removed her wedding ring from her finger yet still wore her husband's dog tags around her neck. He wondered what that signified regarding her perception of her identity.

Perhaps part of Kristina's reluctance to let go wasn't so

much about her husband as much as the fear that without him nothing remained of herself.

None of this was any of his business. But he couldn't shake his deepening fascination with the young military widow. "That's enough for today."

At the strained, husky note in his voice, she glanced at him. "So when do I get to fly this baby?"

He smiled. "One step at a time, Kris. There's always tomorrow."

But early on day three, he received an emergency phone call from Mrs. Savage. There'd been an incident with Jade at school. He needed to come right away.

He dashed off a quick text to Kristina and apologized for canceling their lesson. Jumping into the Jeep, he sped down Seaside Road. His heart drummed in his chest as he raced toward the high school.

Bumping over the small bridge straddling the tidal creek at Quinby, he pulled onto Highway 13. Fear coiled in the pit of his stomach.

Worst-case scenarios floated through his mind. Had someone hurt Jade? Had she punched some overprivileged kid for a remark about her jailbird father?

He'd worked himself into a lather by the time he jerked the Jeep to a standstill at the school.

Mrs. Savage met him at the entrance. "I'm sorry, Mr. Collier. We received her transcripts this morning and revised her schedule accordingly. She didn't take the change well."

"Where's Jade?" He clenched his jaw so tightly his teeth ached. "I want to see her now." A wave of something intense swept over him.

"Canyon? Mrs. Savage?" Kristina barreled inside. "Jade called. She threatened to run away."

"Run away?" He swiveled to the principal. "Where is my niece? What's happened?"

"Jade is in my office. I'm giving her a chance to get her emotions under control after her outburst."

He scowled. "What outburst?"

"Based on her academic performance at her previous school, we feel it's in her best interest to repeat the ninth grade."

Kristina sucked in a breath.

"No." He planted his hands on his hips. "She's a smart girl. She'll catch up. It's not her fault she got behind. Her mother—"

"I'm sorry, Mr. Collier." Mrs. Savage ushered them into the office. "When we spoke with Jade about our decision, she became verbally abusive to the guidance counselor."

Canyon winced. "I apologize for that, Mrs. Savage. But you should've contacted me before telling her. I would've been here—" His eyes scanned the reception area. "Where is my girl?"

Mrs. Savage opened the door to an adjoining room. Jade huddled in a chair opposite the principal's desk. At the sound of his voice, her red-rimmed eyes flicked to his. But her black-coated lips flattened.

"I'm not going back to the ninth grade with those babies." There was defiance in every line of her body. "I won't." But her mouth quivered at the sight of Kristina.

He stepped forward. "Of course you're not going back to the ninth grade. That's not happening."

Mrs. Savage frowned. "Mr. Collier, I explained—"

"She'd be humiliated. I won't put her through that." He placed his hand on Jade's shoulder. "Even if I have to yank her out of this school and put her in a private one."

Jade's eyes cut to his. "But how would you afford—"

"If I have to sell one of the airplanes, I'll make it happen."

Jade's mouth opened and closed.

"Everyone take a breath and calm down." Kristina

cupped the crown of Jade's head with her hand. "Surely there are adjustments that can be made, Mrs. Savage. What about her aptitude scores?"

"Yeah." He broadened his chest. "Jade is extremely intelligent." Jade trembled beneath his hand.

Kristina nodded. "I'm sure Jade can successfully pass the class with extra tutoring."

"If it were only the one class." Mrs. Savage's mouth thinned. "Her grades for tenth grade so far are abysmal, too."

Jade knotted her fingers in her lap. His heart lurched. He'd been here. If it hadn't been for Hap in his life…

Mrs. Savage moved behind her desk. Sitting down, she sifted through a folder. "Jade's standardized scores are actually very high. She's simply not performing to her potential."

He sank into the chair nearest Jade. He reached for her hand. She resisted at first but then unknotted her fingers. "It's hard to concentrate on doing your best in school when you don't know where your next meal is coming from. Believe me, I know."

Over Jade's head, he saw Kristina's blue eyes cloud.

He threaded Jade's hand in his. "That is no longer the case for Jade, I promise you. And I personally guarantee to put in the time to make sure she's up to speed with her classes."

Kristina stroked Jade's hair. "I'll do everything I can to help her, too."

Mrs. Savage's eyebrow rose into a question mark. "You're suggesting Jade juggle her already demanding tenth-grade curriculum on top of trying to complete what she didn't master last year? That's a lot for anyone to handle."

He met the principal's gaze. "Jade won't be handling this

alone. She's got me. We won't let you down, Mrs. Savage, if you'll give us this one chance."

"We? Us?" A smile relaxed Mrs. Savage's stern features. "You believe in her that much?"

His grip tightened on Jade. "I do."

Mrs. Savage scrutinized Jade. "Are you willing to put in the extra effort, Miss Collier? This isn't going to allow you much time for anything else. And there won't be any margin for error. One bad grade…"

Jade's head bobbed so hard her magenta feather fluttered. "I'm not afraid of hard work, Mrs. Savage. Please give me another chance. I won't disappoint you. Or my uncle, either."

He jutted his jaw. "I assure you, Mrs. Savage, Jade will be writing a note of apology to you and the guidance counselor. And apologizing to both of you in person tomorrow."

Jade stiffened.

"I will not allow disrespectful behavior." He never broke eye contact with Mrs. Savage. "My girl is better than that. Colliers are better than that."

Mrs. Savage pursed her lips. "I believe you, Mr. Collier." She pushed away from the desk and rose. "Jade has a test in World History next week."

He let go of Jade's hand and stood, too.

Mrs. Savage came around the desk. "I also expect to see great improvement in her biology lab." She stuck out her hand.

He grasped the woman's hand. "We won't let you down."

"Fine." Mrs. Savage became brisk. "I think we should call it an early day for Jade. She can hit the ground running tomorrow."

But a small, pleased expression lifted the principal's face. And he suddenly wondered whether she'd intended this satisfactory resolution from the start. To test his commitment as a guardian. To prove something to Jade herself.

"Well played, Mrs. Savage," he murmured.

Mrs. Savage kept her gaze lowered as she shuffled a pile of folders on the edge of her desk. But her lips curved. "Why don't you retrieve your books from your locker, Miss Collier, and then go home with your uncle?"

Jade rose. "Yes, ma'am."

"And Jade?"

She paused, midstep, on her way out the door.

"I hope you won't give me a reason to regret this decision."

"No, ma'am. I promise I won't."

After thanking the principal, he and Kristina went into the hall to wait for Jade.

Kristina bit her lip. "I hope you don't think I was interfering, Canyon. But when Jade called so upset, I rushed over here without stopping to think."

He released the breath he hadn't realized he'd been holding. "I'm glad you were here."

She gestured toward the office. "I'm not sure if I helped or not. The situation seemed to be escalating."

He scrubbed his hand over his face. "*I* was escalating. You were the voice of calm. I'm sorry for getting so defensive."

She patted his jacket sleeve. "You have nothing to apologize for. I think you've passed the second hurdle in Parenthood 101." She smiled. "A parent has to be their child's advocate. And you stood your ground on Jade's behalf."

"I wasn't going to let them railroad her. Holding her back would devastate Jade."

"And you did the right thing in refusing to allow Jade to continue with unacceptable behavior." Kristina's eyes welled. "Discipline with a whole lot of love."

His pulse jackknifed. Her approval meant so much.

She punched his bicep lightly. "We'll make a parent out of you yet."

"Not too bad for a sky jockey, huh?"

She blushed. "Now that we know each other better, I'd never call you that again."

Canyon jammed his hands into his pockets. "Better, but not nearly as well as I'd like."

Her cornflower eyes lifted. Their gazes locked. They shared a long look, fraught with awareness and tenderness. A heart-stopping moment.

Then she took a ragged breath and looked away. "I'm pretty good at math. Feel free to send her over anytime."

He gave Kristina a mock salute to ease the tension. "Roger that. Thank you, Kristina."

She turned to go.

"And Kristina?"

She stopped. "Yes?"

"Thanks for being our friend."

A wistful look crossed her features. "Right back at you."

"Shall we try again?"

Kristina gulped. "W-what do you mean?"

"Lesson three. Tomorrow. Same time, same airstrip?"

Her face shadowed. "I—I…" She wheeled toward the exit. "I have to check my schedule. I'll call or leave you a message."

Not what he'd been hoping to hear. For a moment, when they gazed at each other just now, he'd dared to hope that—

He ran his hand over his face. That's what came from hoping and believing. He was an idiot.

Disappointment flooded him as he watched Kristina's Subaru pull out of a visitor space while he waited for Jade. Ten minutes later, she joined him with a bag full of textbooks.

Jade scuffed the toe of her combat boot on the sidewalk. "I apologized in person to the guidance counselor. She gave me this."

He skimmed through the computer printout of assignments. "Good." He held Jade's door open for her.

She scooted inside the Jeep. Going around, he'd inserted the key into the ignition when—

"Did you mean what you said to Mrs. Savage?"

His hand dropped.

Jade stared out the windshield, not making eye contact. "About believing in me?"

"You can be anything you want to be, Jade. And I'd be proud to be a part of making it happen."

Her eyes glistened, but she kept her gaze fastened on the row of cars. "No one's ever believed in me before."

"It only takes one person to make the difference. For me, that person was Hap Wallace." Canyon's throat constricted. "If it hadn't been for him living next door to my grandmother and taking an interest in a sullen, throwaway kid like me, I shudder to think where I'd be now. Most likely dead or—"

"In jail like Beech."

Canyon's mouth twisted. "I tried to be that person for your dad, Jade. I want you to know that. I can't tell you how sorry I am that I failed him. But after what happened, Hap encouraged me to join the Coast Guard. All I'd ever wanted to do was fly planes."

She looked at him then. "You earned your pilot license while still in high school working for Hap?"

He nodded. "The first of several licenses. The Coast Guard offered an escape from the family. Hap died the year before Grandma Eileen. No one was more surprised than me when he left me his airfield. I finished my tour and came home. But by then Grandma was already gone, too."

"So, in a way, you're repaying him. Paying it forward with me."

Canyon clenched the wheel. "It's not a matter of paying it forward. You're family, Jade."

Her eyes watered. "I haven't ever been anybody's girl until now."

Canyon reckoned she hadn't. "I love you, Jade."

With no small sense of amazement, he realized it was true. Mr. Emotional High Wall's heart had been breached. And by this mixed-up teenage niece of his. He saw much of himself in her.

Tears spilled down her cheeks. Before he knew what hit him, she flung herself across the seat. Raising his hands off the wheel, he wasn't sure what to do as she sobbed into his leather jacket.

"I—I love you, too." She draped her arms around his neck. "Nobody's ever told me they loved me."

Another sad fact. Still unsure what to do with his hands, he wrapped his arms around Jade and hugged her back.

"I'm always going to be in your corner, Jade. You and me are in this for the long haul. Pilot and copilot."

She inched back to peer into his face. "Flyboy and Goth Girl?"

"Not quite the call signs I had in mind, but that'll work, I guess." He swiped his hand across his cheek and sniffed. "Allergies must be bad this time of year."

Settling into her seat, she tilted her head. "Ex-Coastie crop dusters aren't allowed to cry, huh?"

He cranked the ignition. "This ex-Coastie aerial application specialist wants lunch. How about hitting Tammy and Johnny's before we hit the books?"

Jade groaned. "Why do I get the feeling you've enrolled me in the Collier version of boot camp?"

He headed for the highway. "Hoo-ah, Seaman Recruit Collier." He fist-pumped the air.

"Ugh…" The back of her head fell onto the headrest, but she raised her arm, too.

Although not as high or as enthusiastically as his.

"Hoo-ah," she grunted.

Canyon grinned. "There's that fighting Collier spirit."

She gave him a sidelong look. "Maybe you should thank Kristina for coming to my rescue. Take her out to lunch tomorrow."

His insides squeezed. "I don't think that's a good idea."

"Why not?"

"Because we're neighbors. Because Gray works for me. Because—"

"'Cause you're a big chicken."

He shook his head. "Don't go getting any foolish notions in your magenta-colored head. Kristina and I aren't going to happen, not the way you're hoping. Good fences make good neighbors."

She rolled her eyes. "There's no fence between her property and yours."

"There's fences that you can't begin to comprehend, Jade."

Her nose wrinkled. "That doesn't make any sense."

"The biggest fence of all is the one Kristina has erected herself. She's a widow." He rapped the side of his thumb against the wheel. "Women like her don't just get over that kind of loss."

"So help her get over it." Jade threw out her hands. "You like her, I know you do. You get funny-looking when she walks in a room. Where's *your* fighting Collier spirit?"

"Funny-looking?" he growled. "And for your information, Miss Know It All, some things can't be changed no matter how you wish they could."

"And some things are worth fighting for, Uncle."

"Stubborn you got in spades."

"I think you need to go for it with Kristina. What've you got to lose?"

He could think of several things—his pride, his mind and, most of all, his heart. But for now, he'd settle for getting Jade off his case. He didn't like being rushed or pushed—another Collier family trait.

"I'll think about what you said."

"Better think fast." She cocked her head. "The good ones don't stay unclaimed long."

Chapter Nine

A few weekends later, nearing dusk, Kristina pulled into a parking space alongside the Kiptohanock square.

Unsure what to expect, she'd nevertheless volunteered to help with the pancake supper. She waved to Gray as he and the youth group unfolded tables and chairs on the green.

Standing on the gazebo steps like a carved figurehead on the prow of a ship, Margaret Davenport supervised the teens, in particular, and everyone else in general. Including Seth Duer, fastening a string of lights around the gazebo railing.

As Kristina approached, he paused long enough to roll his eyes.

Ignoring them, Margaret hastened down the steps and sailed across the square to harangue the Coast Guard auxiliary retirees. They'd made the mistake of loitering a second too long outside the fellowship hall.

Removing a handkerchief from his jeans, Seth wiped his brow. "I'm getting too old to deal with the likes of Margaret Upshur Davenport."

Slipping her keys into her coat pocket, Kristina realized the two must be about the same age. "Margaret is certainly enthusiastic."

"No need to sugarcoat it." He lifted his ball cap and resettled it on his graying head. "Margaret's just plain bossy."

Kristina smiled. "She runs this village with an efficiency corporations would envy."

"She runs this village like it's her own personal kingdom." He crimped the hat brim with his hand. "Still, she's got the town's best interests at heart, I guess."

"What doesn't kill us will cure us?"

He laughed. "Something like that." His mustache drooped. "We've each got battles to fight and wars to overcome."

Kristina's eyes cut to the sixtysomething woman marshaling the retirees into carrying bags of ice out of the church kitchen. "What kind of wars do you mean?"

Seth leaned against the railing, taking a breather. "I wage war against depression. For some, it's addictions and anger. Or grief."

Kristina swallowed.

His gaze slid in Margaret's direction. "For others, letting go of the past. How's your war going, Kristina?"

Shading her eyes with her hand, she contemplated the harbor and the docked watercraft. With the setting of the sun, the breeze had picked up. She was glad she'd brought her coat. "Some days are better than others."

"I hear that."

She shrugged. "It's tricky getting the balance just right."

"I live that, darlin'." He chuckled. "The struggle is real. Daily."

She tucked her hand inside the warmth of her coat to finger Pax's dog tags. "It's hard to let go without losing any of the good stuff. Stuff you don't ever want to forget and yet at the same time…"

"Taking hold of something new."

Kristina played with the cold, rounded edges of the metal. "Exactly."

Seth Duer spoke truth. Time to take another small step forward?

He and Caroline had started GriefShare at the church about a year ago. Her sister-in-law had been quietly urging Kristina to attend since she moved to Kiptohanock.

Kristina took a deep breath. "What night does Grief-Share meet, Mr. Duer?"

"Tuesdays. And it's Seth. Come when you can, darlin'."

"Seth Duer!" Margaret bellowed across the square.

He ducked as if dodging an incoming mortar.

"I don't see any lights blazing yet!" Hands on her ample hips, she glowered. "I want to see lights blazing!"

Seth grunted. "I'd like to set her lights—" But he zagged right as Margaret careened across the square. "Gotta go."

Kristina bit back a laugh.

He tipped his cap. "No rest for the weary." He disappeared behind the gazebo.

Margaret advanced. And following his wise example, Kristina zipped left. Maybe the firefighters needed her help cooking pancakes.

She scooted—okay, she ran—for the open bay of the white-painted brick fire station on the other end of the green.

And almost collided with Canyon, his arms loaded with a stack of paper plates. The clean, soapy smell of him teased her nostrils. She flushed, wondering if he'd witnessed her inelegant flight across the square.

His eyes crinkled. Lines fanned out from his swimming pool eyes. His well-muscled chest convulsed in the effort not to laugh. Apparently he had.

Crossing her arms, she tapped her sneaker on the concrete. "Go ahead. Laugh. You know you want to, flyboy."

His lips twitched. "Retreat the better part of valor, huh?"

She sniffed. "Live to fight another day."

"Is that what you call taking to your heels?"

She raised her fist. "We fight for freedom."

"I can't wait to hear you express that sentiment to Queen

Margaret." He smirked. "I'm sure Jade could give you a good deal on blue face paint."

Kristina laughed. "Your niece brings much-needed color to this town."

"She brings something, all right."

Kristina wagged her finger. "You don't fool me, Canyon Collier." She took the plates from him. "You're so proud of her you can't stand it."

"Yeah, especially after she volunteered me to work this fund-raiser. My former—emphasis on former—best friend Sawyer egged her on."

After the incident at the school, Kristina had only managed to hold out four hours before leaving a message saying she'd meet Canyon at the airfield the next day for another flying lesson.

It had been an amazing few weeks with Canyon Collier in her life. February had rolled into March. She found herself excited about the start of each new day. Because of her flying lesson—the lesson, not the instructor.

That's what she told herself. Repeatedly. Especially when her heart went pitter-patter at sunrise each morning.

Not that mornings were the only time they spent together. She took the kids to school, and he brought them home in the afternoon. They also got into the habit of sharing dinner while everyone helped Jade with her academic load. Kristina enjoyed cooking for a man again.

She tried telling herself it was great to just have an adult conversation. But the truth was, Canyon stirred feelings inside her she'd never believed she'd experience again. And left her heart yearning for more.

Such thoughts were not only futile, but dangerous.

Kristina lifted her chin. "Should I report for kitchen duty?"

In navy blue KFD T-shirts, Sawyer, her brother, Weston, and several other volunteer firefighters flipped pancakes on the griddle in the station kitchen. Clipboard in hand, Jade appeared to be supervising.

"Jade's got that area under control," Canyon mumbled. "Appointed by Queen Margaret herself."

Kristina did a double take. "Jade and Margaret?"

"Hit it off like long-lost sisters. Go figure. Now there's two of 'em. God save us all."

Kristina nudged him. "You probably need supervision."

"So says Jade." But he grinned. "Which are you? Helper or supervisor?"

"Definitely helper."

"Good." He pointed to the long white tables running parallel in the bay. "We're almost ready. Stack the plates on the end. It's a self-service line. I'm on ticket duty. Wanna help me give out change?"

"Sure." She deposited the plates. "All hands on deck for Kiptohanock. And for such a good cause—the BackPack Buddy Food Drive."

He set out a tray of napkin-wrapped utensils. Filling plastic glasses with ice and sweet tea, Dixie, the waitress at the café and her engineer husband, Bernie, waved.

Emerging from the kitchen, Weston handed Kristina a pan of steaming pancakes and gave Canyon the head-up nod guys did. "Canyon."

Canyon responded in like manner. "Weston."

Which in guy talk meant they were cool with each other. As Wes returned to the kitchen, she sensed a hurdle had been overcome between Canyon and the other men.

Grabbing a set of tongs, she began transferring the hot cakes into the empty aluminum trays. "I love the sense of community here."

He adjusted the position of the Sterno burning under the pans. "This program will ensure the kids get one good meal a day over summer break. Until Beech and I came to live with our grandmother, we were them."

Kristina's heart fluttered at the image of a little boy with curly brown hair and sky-blue eyes. A boy and his brother who understood what it felt like to be hungry.

In between getting her flight ready, he'd shared heart-rending glimpses of a chaotic upbringing. And his feelings of being an outsider due to a mother always on the move.

Each time she saw him helping Jade, he also proved—without meaning to—what a good man he was despite his rough beginnings. A man worth knowing.

Worth loving, too?

She frowned and set the lid atop the pan with a clang. Startled, Canyon smiled as he moved to intercept more pancake platters from Wes.

Canyon was proving to be a good friend. Nothing more. There could never be room in her life for anyone else.

There'd been moments, though—like the accidental touch of his hand against her skin. Her pulse accelerated at the memory. An intensity in his gaze.

As if he, too, felt these incredibly wonderful—and frightening—feelings consuming Kristina. She hid her face in the collar of her coat.

Returning, Canyon held the tray steady for her to fill another pan. She kept her focus on the pancakes, not the pilot. Was it hot in here? Maybe she didn't need the coat.

Being with him drowned out everything but the heat of her flushed cheeks and the beating of her heart.

Despite the milling volunteers, her heart raced at his proximity. And as always, she was torn by the conflicting desire to flee and a craving to know what it would be like to kiss him.

Laying down the tongs, she fanned herself with her hand. "I may have to take off this coat."

"Okay…" His brow puckered. "It'll get cold through the open bay when it's finally dark, though."

But to her relief, he headed once more toward the cutout window between the bay and the kitchen.

She ditched the coat in favor of shirtsleeves. Sometimes she wished she could love and be loved again by someone after Pax. Loved by Canyon?

Kristina immediately dismissed the thought as disloyal. Pax deserved her devotion. Not this crop— She gritted her teeth. Not this aerial application specialist.

Canyon arrived with a pitcher of warmed maple syrup. "Last job before we open for business." He leaned over the table and poured the contents into evenly spaced smaller containers.

She bit her lip, trying to shake her melancholy. "It's my first community event."

He glanced up. "Mine, too. Thanks to Sawyer and Jade." He grimaced.

She smiled. "And long past time for you to get your head out of the clouds and overcome your antisocial tendencies."

He played with one of the ladles, allowing the oozing syrup to drip slowly into the vessel.

"Stop messing with that." She swatted his hand. "You're going to spill it on the tablecloth."

The corner of his mouth curved. "There's nothing wrong with having wings, you know."

Kristina's insides puddled. It was so unfair when he looked at her like that. And so hard to think. "Nothing wrong with roots, either."

His eyes went half-mast. "Perhaps people need both. Wings and roots."

Kristina's heart pounded. "Maybe so."

She spotted Margaret, hovering within earshot near the EMS vehicle parked outside the bay.

Reddening, Kristina moved toward the cashier's box on the ticket table. "Customers are arriving."

He dropped into the adjacent folding chair.

"With your Coast Guard background, I'm surprised you haven't been recruited before now. Jade's pulling you out of your splendid isolation."

"And of all places, a firehouse. Irony? Or penance?" He scrubbed his hand over his beard stubble. "I can't decide which."

She frowned as she accepted money from Charlie Pruitt and made change. Canyon handed the deputy sheriff and Evy their tickets for the raffle after the dinner.

Evy pushed her horn-rimmed glasses up the bridge of her nose with her finger. "We're going to eat quick. Margaret told us to relieve you guys so you can eat, too."

Charlie's mouth thinned. "Good to see you performing your civic duty."

The implied *for once* went unspoken. Kristina's eyes ping-ponged between the men. What was with this town and Canyon?

"Don't do me any favors, Pruitt," Canyon growled.

"Sorry," Evy mouthed as she yanked Charlie toward the food.

Kristina made change for a Coastie family. "What was that about?"

He blew out a breath. "Long memories is what that was about."

The crowd kept them busy for the next thirty minutes. Amelia and her family shuffled through the line. Plates in hand, Caroline and Izzie also headed out to the tables on the green. Offering refills, Gray and other teenagers trotted tea pitchers back and forth.

At the next lull, she closed the cash box. "What did you mean about Jade's involvement with the firehouse being irony or penance?"

Canyon slumped. "You don't know?" He shook his head. "You flush the toilet at one end of Kiptohanock, and everyone at the other end soon knows."

"Is this about what happened with Jade's father?"

He stared at her. "You really don't know what Beech did?"

"What he did has nothing to do with you or Jade."

"If only…" He squeezed his eyes shut and opened them. "I'd hate to see you and Gray blacklisted by association with us."

"Small towns," she huffed. "Why can't everyone let bygones be bygones?"

Canyon raked his hand over his close-cropped hair, leaving it disheveled.

She coiled her hands in her lap, lest she give in to the urge to smooth his hair.

"Maybe if I'd been there—but I took off to help Hap make a run in the plane. Beech hung out with a rough crowd who carried a grudge against several locals. That was also the night Brandi told him she was pregnant."

"It was so long ago, Canyon."

"There's no excuse for what he did." Canyon's expression became bleak. "The jury thought so, too. As does the town, and I can't blame them."

"What did Beech do, Canyon?"

His mouth tightened. "Beech set fire to a fishing boat. It burned to the waterline. A family's livelihood, gone up in smoke. And he didn't stop there."

Kristina ached for Canyon and Jade living with this terrible legacy.

"He torched a farmhouse." Canyon's head fell forward. "The fire department was already on scene at the waterfront when they got the call. By the time the crew arrived, the house was engulfed. The guy Beech was so angry with wasn't there. But his pregnant wife and two small children were asleep in their beds."

She gasped. "Oh, Canyon."

"One of the kids didn't make it out." Remembered pain

darkened his eyes. "Our mother screwed up the both of us, but I've never understood how Beech—how he could…" Beads of sweat had broken out on Canyon's forehead. "My brother doesn't even remember setting the house fire."

"And you've spent your life trying to atone for what he did."

"I don't want Jade bearing that burden." Canyon clenched his fist. "Why did Margaret put us in the firehouse?"

Kristina searched for Jade and found her beside the fire engine, chatting with a boy from the football team. Seeing her, too, Gray had gone stock-still at the tea table.

"Have the firefighters been hostile to you or Jade to-night?"

"Actually, no." His eyes shot toward the football jock as he laughed at something Jade said. "Maybe Margaret was right to force the issue."

"Margaret's an interfering busybody." Kristina bristled. "You should be able to tackle the problem in your own way and in your own time."

Chapter Ten

Seated at the ticket table in the fire station, Canyon fidgeted. "My way involves a lot of avoidance. Probably not the best approach if Jade is going to make a life here." He shrugged. "Besides, Margaret has our best interests at heart."

"Best interests?" Kristina blinked at him. "Margaret Davenport?" A brisk wind from the open bay ruffled her crinkly blond hair.

He shifted his focus outside to the twinkling lights of the gazebo in the square. "Margaret was a good friend to my grandmother. Especially after she was diagnosed with dementia when I was stationed in Florida. Margaret looked after her. I owe Margaret big time."

"I didn't realize your grandmother had dementia." Kristina sighed. "Pax's father died young from early-onset Alzheimer's. It's a terrible disease. It was hard letting go."

His heartbeat quickened. Was she starting to put the past behind her? Or was he grasping at straws?

Canyon gulped past the longing clogging his throat. "Dementia brings a helplessness to the patient and family alike. I had to watch from a distance. Margaret was a lifesaver."

Kristina pursed her lips. "That surprises me about Margaret."

"Her bark is worse than her bite."

Kristina cocked her head.

He laughed. "Okay, maybe not. But she's taken Jade and me under her wing—" he rolled his tongue in his cheek "—and I'll take what I can get."

Canyon's smile faded. Taking what he could get. Story of his life.

By eight o'clock, the crowds had departed. The fire truck and EMS vehicles were once more parked where they belonged. Under Margaret's direction, the cleanup crew toted tables and chairs back to the fellowship hall.

It didn't escape his notice only the single men remained behind to help put the kitchen to rights. How many firefighters did it take to unscrew a lightbulb?

More than a few, judging from the number of men clustered around Kristina.

Chagrined, he recalled Jade's words. Should he stake his claim with the rest? He glared through the cutout kitchen window.

But what chance did someone like him have with someone like Kristina? She and Gray deserved far better than anything he could offer. He wasn't in the same league as her late husband.

Yet his stomach knotted at the sight of her with those guys. Futility burned like acid in his throat. She stirred feelings in him that he'd not thought himself capable of.

Leaving him with a hunger for more. For those roots she claimed she preferred. As for his splendid isolation? Between Kristina Montgomery and Jade, that yearning had been smashed to smithereens.

Based on experience, he disliked needing anyone. And despite the strong defensive measures of a lifetime, he was fast coming to need Kristina, Gray and Jade in his life. But needing people only made you vulnerable.

In the end, people always let you down. And he'd already endured just about all the hurt he could carry in one lifetime. So he landed on his fallback emotion rather than acknowledge the pain.

Lips pinched, Canyon handed the cashier's box to Margaret.

Margaret didn't look up as she tallied the receipts. "Those lights aren't going to take themselves off the gazebo."

Jade leaned her chair on its legs. "Can you help Uncle Canyon, Kristina?" she shouted. "Miss Margaret and I are busy here."

Chatting with one of the muscle-bound volunteer firefighters, Kristina jolted. And he detected a distinct gleam in Jade's green eyes.

She winked. "You can thank me later," she whispered.

Flushing, he pivoted on his heel and headed outside.

"Canyon, wait up."

Kristina caught him as he crossed the deserted street. "I didn't realize you needed my help."

"I don't—" He clenched his jaw. "There's work to be done on the square. If you're not too busy."

Her eyes widened. "I'm not too busy."

Canyon stalked toward the lighted gazebo. But some of his frustration seeped away. He bent over the electric outlet.

Her brow creased. "Are you mad at me?"

"Why should I be angry with you, Kristina?"

He pulled the plug. Darkness settled over the square. He waited for his eyes to adjust.

A half-moon silhouetted the town. Dock lights glimmered from the pier. And beyond the village square, the muted glow from residential homes.

She rubbed her arms over the sleeves of her pink sweater. A soft cashmere. Not that he knew firsthand whether the fabric was soft or not.

His mouth dry, he unwound a strand of lights from the railing. "I got this. You don't have your coat."

She frowned.

"You can go inside. I got this," he said.

She didn't move. "You said that already."

Acutely aware of her, every fiber of his being pulsated at her nearness. He swallowed hard. He unplugged the cord from yet another entwined connection.

"I can hold that for you." Her hand brushed across his in the darkness.

He jumped back half a foot. "I don't need—"

"You've made that perfectly clear." She yanked one end of the lights. "Canyon Collier needs help from no one." She quivered. "Especially not from me. A friend."

"A friend?" He abandoned his end of the cord. "Is that how you see things between us? As friends?" He took a step forward.

She took a step back. "Why can't we keep things the way they are? The kids are happy."

His eyebrows rose. "Are you happy, Kristina? Can you ever really be happy holding on to memories of your dead husband? Must get awful cold, especially this time of year."

She held the lights awkwardly between them. "I don't want to talk about Pax."

"Friends or nothing, is it?" He threw out his hands. "Then I choose nothing." He wheeled away from her.

She caught at his leather coat. "Canyon...please."

"What is it you want from me, Kristina? I can't go on this way." He shook his head. "Not knowing how to act when I'm with you. Not able to tell you how I feel when—"

"Don't say anything else." She dropped the strand of lights and seized a fistful of his shirt. "Kiss me." She tugged him closer.

Her breath brushed his cheek. He inhaled the light floral fragrance she wore.

Closing her eyes, she lifted her face in the moonlight.

He fought the desire to lean into her. This was a bad idea. In so many ways.

He was sure it wasn't him she wanted. She wanted to prove something to herself.

She wanted to feel alive again. And Canyon was the closest man available. A man she could trust. A man safe enough to kiss.

This would not end well if he kissed her. This could never end well for them, considering her heart was buried six feet under.

"Canyon…"

His heart lurched. He could no more deny his feelings for her than he could deny the instinct to breathe. Why was he fighting her? Why was he fighting himself?

Canyon cupped her face in his hands. His mouth found hers. Hesitancy gone, he kissed her.

And she kissed him back. Her hands wrapped around his neck, she melted into his arms.

"Kristina, I—"

"Don't." She staggered back and fumbled for the chain around her neck.

That chain… He gritted his teeth. "Kris, we need to talk." He reached for her.

She wrenched out of his reach. "This isn't right." She braced against the railing. "Paxton is the great love of my life."

Is…

"You wouldn't have kissed me like that unless—"

"There's always only been Pax." She gripped the dog tags. "I can't—"

"You mean you won't." Blinding anger at her stubbornness shook him. "You won't even try."

He'd hoped—oh, how he hoped once she felt even a measure of what he felt for her, that she'd…that she would what?

Fall into his arms? Declare her forever love for him? Want a life with him?

He was the biggest kind of fool. She was lonely. He was lonely. That was it.

Shaking like a beech tree in a gale-force wind, she rubbed the metal tags between her fingers. "I'm sorry, Canyon."

He steeled his heartbeat to settle. To go numb once more. To soar above the pain. "I'm the one who's sorry. I should've never..."

"I asked you to kiss me."

He turned away. "So now we both know."

"I never meant to hurt you."

He picked up the tangled string of lights. "No one ever means to hurt anyone."

But it happened. Over and over. For him, at least.

He was an idiot. Had he learned nothing from his grand-mother and his mother? Happily-ever-afters weren't meant for Colliers.

"Let me help you with the lights. It's the least—"

"If I can't have the most with you, Kristina Montgomery, then I don't want the least. Not from you."

A glitter of tears welled in her eyes. "I'm just so confused. I—"

He cleared his throat. "I think it's probably better if we give each other some space."

She shivered and hugged herself. "If that's what you want."

"Not even close to what I want. But maybe what we both need right now."

She scanned the gazebo. "But the lights—"

"Like I said, I got this. Leave me alone, Kristina." His voice hitched. "Please."

Without another word, she walked away. Away from him. Away from a life with him.

His heart felt as dead as the only man she'd ever love.

Chapter Eleven

Kristina's mornings were free once again. Over the next month, she made good on her promise to attend GriefShare.

Other than introducing herself, she didn't have much to say. She was there to learn about the grief process. She saved contemplation of her own situation for the wee hours of increasingly lonely nights.

As for her nonexistent relationship with Canyon? At thoughts of him, her mind grew as foggy as the morning mist over the marsh.

Jade spent after-school hours studying at Kristina's house. Joint carpool continued. Yet Kristina didn't see much of the aerial aviation specialist as March blossomed into April.

Instead, Gray spent his weekends and afternoons at the airfield learning every single mechanical part on every single aircraft. At Canyon's insistence, before he'd allow the boy into a cockpit.

She found herself watching the sky for Canyon's plane as the growing season began. And because she couldn't seem to help herself, listening for the droning sound of his engine when he returned each afternoon.

The sight of the yellow wings sent a double shaft of pain and pleasure into her heart. How it could be both, she didn't understand.

But nothing stopped her from returning to the kitchen

window each day. Searching the sky. Scanning the horizon. Until her hope was rewarded.

Slowly, the soil warmed. The earth was reborn. Spring enveloped the Shore as winter lost its grip. And life was restored.

Her garden pulsed with vibrancy. Foliage unfurled on the trees between her house and the airfield. Apple green—the color of spring in its first flush. Reminding her of the spring when Pax came into her life all those years ago.

That season forever past. But somehow, this year the flowers seemed startlingly vivid. She wasn't sure why.

Her garden bloomed with reckless exuberance. Reckless because she feared the potential of a killing frost to stunt new growth.

So she hunkered in her bungalow. But no more flying lessons. No more coffee or meals. No more shared anything with Canyon.

At church, she kept her distance from Canyon. And Canyon kept his. Which was exactly what she wanted. Wasn't it? Then Margaret Davenport called.

"I need your expertise. We have an emergency wedding situation. Gloria Fitchett's granddaughter absolutely has to get married this Friday."

"Friday?" She clutched the phone. "As in tomorrow? What about the Easter egg hunt on Saturday?"

"Exactly why the wedding has to take place on Friday." Margaret's tone became clipped. "The fiancé just received his orders to ship out next week."

"I don't understand why this involves—"

"He's stationed across the bay in Norfolk. The wedding was set for June, but with his sudden deployment, they don't want to wait." Margaret's voice softened. "Kristina, can you come to Inglenook and help me assemble a bridal bouquet or not?"

She glanced around her kitchen. The kids were at

school—she'd started thinking of Jade almost as her own. Her day stretched before her. She was sick of her own company and her muddled thoughts. Maybe she could use a distraction.

"Kristina," Margaret cajoled. "I figured, being a military wife, you would understand."

"I'm a military widow," she corrected.

Saying the words carried a twinge of pain but no longer the dart of grief she'd come to expect. She blew out a tentative breath, relieved and saddened at the same time.

Margaret wasn't finished with her sales pitch. "You understand better than most the demands the military makes on a family."

That she did. Besides, how could she refuse an invitation to see the much-lauded Inglenook?

"I'll come."

"Excellent." Satisfaction dripped across the line. "I assume you know the way."

She rolled her eyes at the ceiling. Typical Margaret—the center of her own universe. As if anyone could not know the way to Inglenook.

"I'll see you in thirty minutes, Margaret."

Margaret sniffed. "Not a moment longer. I don't like to be kept waiting." Then she hung up.

Kristina groaned. This had the makings of a trying day. Margaret had a way of putting a person's back up. Or at least hers. So she deliberately dawdled.

She put away the laundry. She lingered over her grocery list. But sneaking a peek at the clock, she couldn't endure the tension. It'd take a braver woman than Kristina to incur Margaret Davenport's displeasure.

"Coward…" But she headed for the car.

The traffic this time of year was nonexistent. She slowed as she approached town. Circling the square, she averted her eyes from the gazebo. She continued south to the other end of Seaside Road. A few country miles later, she sighted Inglenook's pillared brick entrance.

Kristina braked in the middle of the road, letting the car idle. Fields and woods lay on both sides of the road. Not another home in sight. Isolated, even for the sparsely populated Shore.

She gulped, suddenly glad for her small, comfy bungalow. Margaret must get extremely lonely out here by herself. But on second thought, perhaps not.

Margaret was too busy running Friends of the Library and the church altar guild. Probably running the Commonwealth of Virginia, too.

To the best of her knowledge, Margaret didn't have any children or grandchildren. Not for the first time, Kristina thanked God for Gray.

Making a left, she followed the gravel drive around the bend. At the straightaway, she steered through the grove of trees lining the drive. The three-story brick Georgian rose from the landscape.

"Wow." She stopped the car again, impressed despite herself.

Inglenook surpassed everything she'd heard. A colonial manor house. Margaret must rattle around in this huge structure.

Kristina veered around the circular fountain and parked. Clamshells crunched beneath her flats as she made her way to the massive oak door.

Jeans and her oversize gray pullover weren't exactly appropriate for such grand surroundings. But she reminded herself this was Margaret's idea. She was doing the woman a favor. Appropriate or not, Margaret could like it or lump it.

Before she could knock, the door flew open.

"Honestly, Kristina…" Margaret crossed her arms. "What took you so long?"

Kristina's gaze cut to her wristwatch. She was—despite her dawdling—three minutes early.

Margaret turned away, leaving her to follow. "Don't just stand there. We've got work to do."

Kristina stepped across the threshold into what could've passed for a wood-paneled great hall of an English country estate.

"Shut the door, please. The house is drafty enough."

Margaret disappeared beyond the carved mahogany staircase into the rear of the house. Hurrying after her, Kristina found herself in a chintz-covered sitting room.

Tall windows and French doors led to a tranquil view of an expansive lawn with a magnificent view of the tidal creek. Beyond the marsh grass, the creek spilled into what must be the Machipongo Inlet.

"It's lovely, Margaret."

The older woman shrugged. "Eighteenth century. My people were one of the early families." She handed Kristina a plastic bucket partially filled with water. Margaret placed a willow basket containing a set of clippers on her own arm.

Kristina tried not to gape at the crown moldings. "In the same family all these generations…"

Margaret stopped, her hand on the French door. "We married well, if not wisely. Not so good a bargain in the long run. I trust you will make a better choice than I did."

Eyebrows raised, she followed Margaret outdoors. They crossed a flagstone terrace and headed into a shaded bower of ancient boxwoods and crape myrtles. No wonder Inglenook won Garden of the Year every year.

At the end of the twisting trail, they came to a clearing full of yellow and orange daffodils nodding in a sweet spring breeze.

Her breath hitched at the loveliness of the meadow. "How beautiful."

Margaret took out the clippers. "I trust you'll know how

best to arrange these into a bridal bouquet. Feel free to gather anything else you need."

Kristina did a slow 360, taking in the view. "The eucalyptus over there for greenery and the trailing ivy..."

Margaret snipped the vines. "You have an eye for floral composition."

Kristina blinked. "Thank you."

"You should open your own shop. Kiptohanock needs a florist. Do what you love."

Hope momentarily surged, then flickered. "I'm an accountant, Margaret."

"You open your own florist shop, and you'll have plenty of opportunities to use your accounting."

"I really don't see that happening in my future."

Margaret balanced the basket on her arm. "And how do you envision your future here?" She sniffed, her patrician nose high in the air. "Unless you're not serious and only sparking with Eileen Collier's grandson to pass the time."

Stung, she stepped back. "Sparking?"

"Dating." Margaret swept toward the house. "Or whatever it's called these days."

"We're not..." Speaking to Margaret's back, Kristina trailed after her with the flower-laden bucket. "We're friends." Or at least they had been.

In a thoroughly modern kitchen, Margaret unloaded the flowers onto a granite countertop. "I heard he was giving you flying lessons. He doesn't do that for just anyone."

"How did you—"

"Nothing's a secret on the Shore for long."

Kristina recalled Canyon's comment about toilets flushing. The grapevine of Kiptohanock had struck again.

"Canyon was helping me get over my fear of flying so I'd give my permission for him to teach Gray."

Margaret separated the blooms from the greenery. "I have no doubt you two could teach each other a lot."

Kristina wasn't sure what to say to that.

"Once you're ready to let go of the past and move forward into the future." Margaret tilted her head, stem in hand. "Case in point, the florist shop." Her blue-green eyes sharpened. "And your dead husband."

Kristina's mouth thinned. "I thought I came to arrange flowers, not be psychoanalyzed."

"The psychoanalysis is an added bonus. I mainly wanted to determine your intentions regarding Canyon."

Kristina stiffened. "Canyon is a good man. Trying to do right by his niece. He's been a good friend to my son, who needs a male mentor in his life."

"And you?" Margaret's gaze locked on to hers. "What do you need?"

"I…" What did she need? "I still need a job. But here I've found a fresh start. A place to belong."

"All the more reason to open the shop. Put the past behind you. But what about Canyon?"

Kristina squared her shoulders. "I realize with his family's reputation, most people—"

"Margaret Upshur Davenport is not most people. You misunderstand me."

Kristina gritted her teeth. "I can take care of myself."

"I ask your intentions, not because I'm afraid of Canyon hurting you." Margaret's eyes flashed. "But because I want to make sure you don't hurt him if a future with him isn't something you foresee. The boy doesn't need more hurt in his life."

That "boy" was thirty-eight years old. And apparently the dragon lady of Inglenook had appointed herself his personal guardian.

Margaret thrust a bunch of flowers across the counter at her. "Let's work while we talk. We've also got boutonnieres and the maid of honor's bouquet to assemble."

They worked side by side while Kristina tried to process her thoughts.

"Eileen Collier and my mother were schoolgirls here during the last world war."

Kristina gave Margaret a sideways glance. She wondered where this was headed. Margaret always had an agenda.

"You wouldn't have recognized our little village during the war years. Its heyday ended with the stock market crash. The steamships stopped coming. And the railroad no longer brought steel magnates south to hunt and fish."

"How do you—You can't be that old."

Margaret's austere features lifted. "Thank you for the compliment. I think."

She reddened. "I meant…"

"My mother and Eileen used to reminisce about those days when the town came back to life. The village bustled with civilian and military personnel."

"Was that when the airstrip next to my house was built?"

Margaret smiled. "Created by the Civilian Air Patrol. The CAP flew daily patrols over the barrier islands."

"Why?"

"Most Americans don't realize how vulnerable the Eastern Seaboard was to invasion, especially during the first few years of war. Packs of German submarines roamed the coastal waters."

Kristina wished she'd asked her grandparents about their war memories before they died. "My grandfather, the final lighthouse keeper on the Neck, must've had a bird's-eye view of the U-boats."

Margaret's smile dimmed. "The airstrip is how Canyon's grandmother Eileen met civilian pilot Freddie Collier."

Kristina cocked her head. "Why am I getting the feeling this doesn't have a happy ending?"

"Because it doesn't."

Margaret handed her a roll of floral tape to bind the

stems together. "He and his best buddy, a 'been here, 'born here pilot, Hap Wallace, palled around with my mother and Eileen. Eileen fell in love with Freddie. Like many CAP pilots, when the imminent threat was over, he and Hap enlisted in the Air Force and saw combat."

"I've heard Canyon speak of Hap Wallace. He returned unharmed?"

"Freddie, too. After the war, they became partners in a crop-dusting business and bought the decommissioned airfield. Freddie married Eileen and moved into your bungalow."

"Is there a *but* coming?"

Margaret pulled a spool of yellow ribbon from a drawer. "Let's use this to finish the bouquet. We must also make additional bows for the church pews."

Kristina could tie bows in her sleep. She made loops of the ribbon. "What happened to Eileen's happily-ever-after?"

Margaret withdrew a container of yellow rosebuds from the refrigerator. "From the florist in Onancock. You could grow your own roses and have them available for customers year-round—"

Kristina sighed, long and loud.

The older lady tidied her workspace. "When the Korean War broke out, over Eileen's objections, Freddie Collier rejoined the Air Force."

Kristina thought about her fears every time Pax had deployed. "I can understand that."

"Eileen was a 'been here through and through. Not Freddie. He was the originator of the Collier wanderlust."

Kristina fluffed the ribbon loops into a bow. Canyon's grandfather sounded like Pax.

"Freddie had a need for speed and a hankering to go places. An often fatal combination. Eileen was pregnant with Canyon's mother by then, too."

Her sympathy for Eileen Collier rose. She knew the hardship of single parenting during deployment.

Margaret adjusted the angle of a stem in the bouquet. "I always say there's two kinds of people on the Shore."

Kristina tied a love knot on the cascading bow she'd created for the bridal bouquet. "The 'been here, 'born heres and the rest of us 'come heres."

Margaret looked up. "I stand corrected. There's three kinds of people on the Shore." She lifted her index finger. "The 'been heres who never want to leave...'"

"Like you and Eileen."

Margaret ticked off her fingers, counting. "...the 'been heres who can't wait to leave—"

"Like Canyon's mother, Amber."

Margaret continued as if without interruption. "—and the 'come heres. Who get here and never want to leave."

"Like me."

Margaret gave her an imperious look. "Obviously, or I wouldn't be wasting my time with you."

Kristina's mouth opened and closed.

Margaret surveyed their handiwork. "Gloria's granddaughter will be so pleased at what we've been able to put together for the wedding."

"What happened to Freddie, Margaret?"

"His plane slammed into some unpronounceable North Korean mountain. His body was never recovered, and Eileen Collier never accepted his death. She believed one day he'd return."

"That's very sad."

"It was tragic. Eileen pined over her dead husband till the day she died, nearly sixty years later. Never letting go, never moving on. Never allowing her neighbor, Hap Wallace—who'd loved her since they were children—to ever become more than a good friend."

Kristina tried to swallow past the sudden lump lodged in her throat.

"Cost them both a lifetime of happiness. Not to mention what living in the past did to Canyon's mother."

Kristina reflected on Gray's frustration with her inertia. And mired in grief, her frustration with herself. Although she was beginning to wonder if it was grief that kept her from going forward with her life—or something else.

Margaret fiddled with an errant blossom. "It mixed up the child. Made Amber feel sorry for herself. Made her feel inadequate. Eileen struggled against the guilt that if she'd somehow been enough, Freddie would've given up his love affair with airplanes and settled down for good."

Kristina suddenly felt an increasing pressure in her chest. Guilt. Was that her problem? Or did the insecurity stem from other issues?

"Mother said no one could've kept Freddie pinned to earth. As futile as trying to hold the wind in your hands."

Again like Pax… She felt a wave of dizziness.

"Misplaced guilt. As if it was her fault he lost control of the airplane and died. Freddie Collier was a charming, elusive, emotionally unavailable man. He loved Eileen— Mother truly believed—as much as he was capable of loving anything without wings."

Wings and roots… Canyon's words played in her head.

"But Amber was like Freddie. Flighty, charismatic, prone to wander. After high school, she left Kiptohanock and never returned. Except for the one time she came to dump two small boys on Eileen."

Kristina probed the discarded piles of leaves on the counter for her keys. "Why did you decide to tell me all this?"

Margaret's carefully plucked eyebrows rose. "Canyon doesn't need a woman stuck in the past like Eileen. Or someone as emotionally unstable as his mother. He needs the real deal from you or not at all."

"Canyon and I are friends, Margaret." Which might no longer be true. "Men and women can be just friends."

Margaret's eyes narrowed. "How long has your husband been dead? Two years?" Her nose wrinkled. "If you're determined to wear widow's weeds for the rest of your life, Kristina, don't take Canyon into the grave with you."

Kristina went rigid. "You have no right to tell me how to feel or not feel. You have no idea what it's like to lose a husband."

"There's all kinds of ways to lose a husband. You don't have a monopoly on heartache."

Kristina had to get out of here. She wasn't going to listen to—

"Please don't hurt him or that purple-haired girl of his. He's not as tough as he likes to pretend. I hope you'll stop running from him and embrace this new possibility."

Kristina clenched her empty fists. "None of this is any of your business, Margaret."

"Despite the cocky pilot bravado, he's never put his heart out there for anyone until you. This push-pull thing you've got going with Canyon isn't fair. To you or him or to those kids."

"I haven't…"

But that's exactly what she'd done at the gazebo after the pancake supper, wasn't it?

Margaret's face took on a wistful expression. "You'll always miss your first love, Kristina. For everyone's sake, miss him always, but let him go."

Hadn't Caroline said almost the same thing to her weeks ago? But Kristina couldn't—she wasn't ready. Yet no matter how she tried to hold on, her memories of Pax were fading.

Like trying to hold the wind in her hands? She squeezed her eyes shut and swayed.

Already she struggled to remember the exact sound of his laugh. The idea of losing her connection with Pax terrified her.

She couldn't breathe. She had to get out of here or... Where were her—

Her hand trembling, Kristina fished out her car keys. "I think we're done here, Margaret."

"Please think on what I've shared with you. I believed you ought to know." Margaret propped her elbows on the counter. "The guild is meeting this afternoon to decorate the sanctuary for the wedding. You'll be there?"

The woman had a lot of nerve...

"We're counting on you, Kristina. You're invaluable to the people who know you, whether you realize it yet or not."

Kristina whirled and ran for the front door. Getting out while she could. How dare Margaret lecture her on overcoming her grief?

But jumping into her car, she sped down the long gravel drive. And she couldn't shake the truth of Margaret's words. Nor Gray's.

Was this about her and her identity? Or about grief? As for Canyon, was her heart trying to tell her a truth her head wasn't ready to hear?

Perhaps it was time to say goodbye to the past and to Pax. But how did she let go? What if she wasn't brave enough?

She shivered at an even more disturbing thought. What would she become—what would become of any of them— if she didn't?

Chapter Twelve

Kristina held the hanger under her chin. "What about this dress, Jade?"

At Jade's surprising request, she'd taken the girl to a secondhand boutique near the waterfront in Onancock. The shop specialized in exclusive party wear consigned by wealthier 'come heres on the Shore.

Jade tilted her head, studying the cocktail dress. Kristina's third attempt. With its swirling geometric colors, the dress had a retro '70s look. And gave Kristina a slight headache.

The teenager's gorgeous green eyes narrowed. "No."

Kristina held back a sigh and replaced the hanger on the sale rack.

"It's not right for me." Jade's hands fluttered. "I'm sorry to be a pain. But the dress doesn't feel like me."

Which encapsulated both the joy and trouble of the adolescent journey. Defining yourself. Once she married Pax, she'd defined herself as a military wife and later as Gray's mother.

Or had she simply become the woman Pax needed her to be? She'd lost herself when he died. Who was Kristina without him?

Jade perused the other items in her size. "It's not easy deciding who I want to be."

Again, Kristina could relate. Her life with Pax was over.

The military wife she'd been—and she'd been a good one, if she did say so herself—was finished.

Time to step into a new persona. Do a remake of herself—of the person she wanted to be. But easier said than done.

Jade held out a soft chiffon concoction. "I kinda like this one… What do you think?"

A moss-green color. "It matches your eyes."

Jade worried her lower lip with her teeth. "Do you think it will make me look like a girl?"

Kristina blinked. "You are a girl, honey. A beautiful girl."

"I don't want to look trashy." Jade fingered the cold-shoulder neckline. "Like Brandi."

Kristina's stomach clenched, saddened for Jade's lack of relationship with her mother. "I think it's elegant and classy. Like you, Jade."

"Do you think Gray would like it?"

So that's how the wind blew these days. Kristina smiled. "I think he would."

Jade raised her chin. "He hasn't asked me to go to the dance. What do you think he's waiting for?"

Uh-oh. An adolescent land mine. One false step and kaboom.

"Gray's shy around girls."

Jade rolled her eyes. "Tell me something I don't know."

Kristina moistened her lips. "He feels very inexperienced when it comes to you."

"Gray thinks I'm experienced? Like Brandi?" Her nostrils flared. "That's not who I am."

She thrust the dress at Kristina.

Kristina sucked in a breath. "That's not what I meant, honey."

Jade's eyes narrowed to emerald slits. "What did you mean, then?"

"I meant that because you're older than him, you're more sophisticated."

"True." Jade sniffed. "He's only a lowly freshman. And a geek, no offense. If you know what I mean."

Jade's mouth quirked, taking the sting out of her words. Reminding Kristina of Canyon with his endearing grin.

She decided not to take offense. "I do know what you mean, Jade."

A full-fledged smile, teeth and all, blazed. Granting Kristina a clear vision of why her son was so fascinated by the intriguing Jade Collier. Colliers possessed an abundance of charm. And apparently the Montgomerys possessed a weakness for their charm.

Jade's stance softened. "Gray's smart, and he's very sweet."

She held the dress against Jade. "Not too short. Or too low cut either. But try it on first."

Jade grimaced. "Canyon made you say that, didn't he?"

"As his stand-in on this shopping expedition, I take my parental duties seriously."

Jade took possession of the hanger. "Canyon's the best dad I never thought could be mine." She shuffled toward the curtained dressing area. "My uncle is smart, too. He's also sweet, if you'd give him a chance."

Kristina pretended to find the button on her denim jacket mesmerizing. Romantic advice from a sixteen-year-old? She reckoned she had it coming.

"There's something else kind of wonderfully strange." Jade stuck her head out of the changing room. "Somehow I think Canyon was always meant to be my dad."

Kristina's gaze lifted.

Jade's eyes glistened. "Like it was just a matter of time until we found each other. A God thing."

Kristina's throat constricted.

"Please don't hurt him, Kristina." Jade's face became earnest. "Please give him and yourself a chance."

"I wish I was ready to say what you want to hear, Jade." She curled her hand around the strap of her purse. "But I can't," she whispered.

Jade's lips flatlined. "Nobody waits forever." She reached for the curtain. "And you can tell your son the same."

With a jerk, she twitched the curtain closed. Shutting Kristina out.

On Saturday, Kristina put the finishing touches on the floral arrangement for the Palm Sunday service. Thanks to word of mouth, the PTA moms had asked her to do the corsages for the spring dance next weekend. She'd contacted a wholesale vendor and now was going to make a tidy profit. Suddenly, the idea of owning a florist shop didn't seem so ridiculous.

She'd be providing a much-needed service to the community. Kiptohanock needed a florist. It was becoming clearer every day in her heart of hearts she was florist material. One more piece of the puzzle as to who the real Kristina was meant to be.

Do what she loved, Margaret had said. Great advice. But she refused to think about what else Margaret had advised.

For the umpteenth time this afternoon, though, Gray trudged into the kitchen. A sports drink. A snack. A cookie. One excuse after the other.

When he offered to wash the lunch dishes, she knew something was up. To the best of her knowledge, he hadn't asked Jade to the dance and had no intention of doing so.

But he'd hovered all day, and she doubted it was because of a sudden, overwhelming interest in flowers.

She stopped working on a ribbon and eyed him as he

slouched against the refrigerator. "Is there something I can help you with, son?"

"You've got a nice way with bows, Mom."

"I thought you'd be working at the airfield. Your first semi-solo flight is Monday, right?"

He propped his elbows on the kitchen island. "Canyon's taking aerial photos of a beach resort near Cape Charles this morning."

Spotting a misplaced stem, she made an adjustment. Gray rapped his fingers in a staccato beat on the counter.

Kristina glanced at him. "Talked to Jade lately?" She fiddled with a blossom.

He shrugged. "I like the corsages with the yellow roses best."

She laid her palms on the counter. Realization dawned. "Did you want to place an order, Gray?"

"I might be in the market for flowers." He wouldn't meet her gaze. "If I decide I want to go to the dance, that is."

His first dance. A big step for her socially gawky son. She sent a swift prayer heavenward for what she ought to say. And more importantly, what she ought not to say.

Dealing with a teenager required employing the same delicacy as tiptoeing through tulips.

"That's wonderful, Gray." She kept her tone light and fixed her attention on sweeping up stray bits of greenery.

"It would be, except…"

Wait for it… She kept her head down and her hands busy.

He blew out a breath. "Thing is, I don't know how to dance."

Should she offer to teach him? Should she let him ask her first?

"You and Dad used to dance."

Her lips curved in a sweet remembrance of an Officers' Ball in San Diego. And for the first time, the memory of

Pax held no pain, only a fond recollection. As if the memory belonged to someone else or to another lifetime.

"I wondered if maybe you'd teach me how to dance." Gray's brow furrowed. "So I don't make a fool out of myself and crush her toes or anything."

She didn't have to guess who the her was. "Have you asked Jade to go with you?"

He pushed away from the island. "I haven't made up my mind to go yet."

"You want a dance lesson before you commit yourself?"

His Adam's apple bobbed in his throat. "Kind of."

She dried her hands on the kitchen towel. "Sure."

He gaped. "You'll teach me?"

"Tell me when and where."

"Like, how about now?"

Kristina nodded. "Help me clear a space in the living room." She swiped her phone, searching for an appropriate playlist. "Fast or slow?"

"Both," he grunted and moved the coffee table next to the hearth.

"No problem." Propping the phone on the mantel, she hit Play. MC Hammer's "Can't Touch This" blared.

Gray's mouth dropped open. "Seriously, Mom?"

"Just feel the rhythm with your body." She demonstrated a move she hadn't employed since college. "Don't worry about your feet. Just move."

He pumped his arms and threw out his elbows. Narrowly missing the lamp on the end table. "Like this?"

She bit the inside of her cheek. Her dear son resembled a cross between a squawking chicken and a snake shedding its skin. But he grinned and hammed it up for her benefit.

By the time the playlist segued to "I Like to Move It," she laughed so hard she doubled over. When "Everybody Dance Now" came on, she flapped her wings and joined Gray in his impromptu chicken dance.

They were both too busy clucking and strutting around to hear the screen door squeak. Too busy laughing until—

"Can anybody join the dance party, or is this a mother-son thing?"

She froze midmotion.

A crooked smile on his ruggedly handsome face, Canyon lolled against the door frame between the living room and kitchen.

She squeezed her eyes shut, wishing she could sink into the floorboards. *God, please. Take me now.* Of all the humiliating... But her heart went into a tango.

Kristina opened her eyes to drink her fill of him. The blue shirt—same hue as his eyes—hung unbuttoned and untucked over a white T-shirt. For once his head was bare of the usual ball cap. His beard stubble was more pronounced, and shadows clouded his face.

She'd ached for a glimpse of him over the last few weeks. She'd missed him more than she'd believed possible.

His sleeves, rolled to his elbows, revealed his tanned, corded forearms. "Don't let me interrupt." Canyon's deep voice produced tiny sparks along her skin. "Great moves, both of you."

She swallowed. "What are you doing here?"

Canyon's eyes cut to her son. "Gray texted me. Said he needed to get a part for the truck from the automotive store this afternoon." Leaning against the wall, he crossed one booted foot over the other. "I had no idea I'd be interrupting—"

"You're not interrupting. We were just finish—"

"Mom..." Gray's brown eyes gleamed. "You said you'd teach me slow dancing, too."

"Uh..." She moved toward the farthest corner. "You go with Canyon. Maybe—"

"Don't mind me." Unfolding from the wall, Canyon dropped into the recliner. "I can wait."

She glared at him.

Cocking his head, he gave her another lopsided smile. "I wouldn't miss this for the world."

Her hand flitted to her hair. When was the last time she'd combed it? This morning? She wrapped her arms around the ratty old sweater she wore.

Gray retrieved her phone from the mantel. "I need to find slower dance songs."

"Let me." Canyon fished his phone out of his pocket. "How about we start with a waltz? Keep it simple."

Gray broadened his skinny chest. "I need simple."

Kristina fought the urge to run upstairs. She needed to at least brush her hair. But who was she kidding?

She needed a makeover—probably liposuction. And possibly, after Canyon had seen her in this bedraggled state, psychological counseling.

Canyon held up his cell. "How about this?"

Strains of "I'll Be Seeing You" floated into the air. Canyon and his big band obsession.

Gray's eyes bored into hers. "Mom?"

So she resigned herself to taking one for Team Gray.

Moving closer to her son, she placed her hand on his shoulder. And took his hand in hers. "Put your other hand around my waist…"

Standing next to him, she had to raise her gaze to meet his. Her heart tugged at the realization of how her little boy had matured. He was already as tall as his dad and still growing.

Gray's eyes glinted with a suspicious mischief. "Now what?"

She straightened her posture. "We make a box."

"A what?"

Canyon got out of the chair. "Trace a square with your steps. One corner to the next. All four sides."

"Like this." Taking a step backward, she dragged Gray's

body forward. "But you're supposed to lead." She towed Gray toward the next corner of the imaginary box.

Canyon had resumed his watchful, relaxed perch against the wall. "Your mom has to do this backward and in heels."

She smiled, recognizing the quote from Ginger Rogers. Like an automaton, Gray completed the square. "Loosen up, hon," she whispered.

"I'm not feeling it." Gray scratched his head. "Maybe if you guys showed me how it's supposed to be done…?"

She went rigid. "W-what?"

Canyon's mouth fell open.

He looked at Gray. Then at Kristina, whose eyes had gone deer-in-the-headlights wide. His gaze shifted once more to Gray.

And noted a distinct gleam in the boy's eyes. They'd been played. By a teenager.

"Make a box…" Gray's voice took on the cajoling tone of a symphony conductor forced to deal with the musically challenged. "Four corners. Move your feet."

Gray put his hand in Canyon's back and shoved him a foot closer to his mother. Canyon almost stumbled into her.

Her son hefted her arm like a piece of driftwood. "Put your hand on his shoulder, Mom." Kristina remained mute but unresisting.

When Gray let go, her hand plunked on top of Canyon's shoulder. He flinched.

"Take her hand, Canyon." Gray sighed. "Do I have to do everything? Put your hand on her waist, Coastie."

Canyon's tongue molded to the roof of his mouth.

Her son sighed again, the sound trickling through his lips like they tried all the patience to be had in the world. "Take Canyon's hand, Mom."

Gulping, she complied. Arm in arm, they stared at each other. So awkward. Gray did a quick search on Kristina's phone. When he hit Play, Doris Day's rendition of "When I Fall in Love" floated to the beams of the bungalow.

Canyon's gut tightened. Bittersweet and apropos. Considering his hopeless, helpless love for Gray's mother.

He took a deep breath to replenish his suddenly oxygen-starved lungs. He'd missed her so much… Staying away had taken every ounce of willpower he possessed.

Gray planted his hands on his hips. "Come on, you guys. Move it or lose it."

Canyon believed he'd already lost any chance for Kristina's love. But with her so close to him…maybe this was the only opportunity he'd ever have to hold her in his embrace.

"Ready?" he whispered.

Kristina's breathing became more rapid. "As I'll ever be."

Her soft skin warm in his callused, work-roughened hand, his feet moved of their own volition. And she fell into step with him.

Those beautiful china-blue eyes of hers never left his. In their shimmering depths, he lost himself. Felt himself drowning. And didn't care.

She felt so right in his arms. So good and lovely and true. As if she'd always belonged there. As if only now, he'd come home to the place he was always meant to be.

Again and again, they formed the box waltz with their steps. The words flowed around him. Would Kristina ever love him the way he loved her? The music swelled and crescendoed.

Their gazes locked. An awareness of him filled her eyes. She trembled. And with a sharp intake of breath, she halted. The love song played on without them.

"Why did you guys stop?"

"I—I think that's enough." Her pink-tinted lips trembled. "Don't you, Canyon?"

He dropped his hand from her waist and stepped away.

He didn't think it was enough. It would never be enough until her love was truly his forever.

But he stood about the same chance of her loving him one day as a pig had of flying. Taking another step backward, he retreated toward the relative safety of the door frame.

This was insane. No good could ever come from loving a woman who'd never stop loving her dead husband. He had only to recall Hap's lifelong silent anguish.

And if he didn't get out of this room—away from Kristina—this very moment, he was going to lose all pride. Embarrass them both. Lose any chance of remaining her friend.

Because friendship was all he'd ever have with Kristina. It was best he accepted the terms of any continued relationship with her.

He backpedaled toward the kitchen. "Gotta go."

She didn't move.

"Wait." Frowning, Gray started after him. "Can I go, too?"

Canyon bolted for the back door. "Another time," he called over his shoulder.

The door banged against the siding in his haste to get away from his grandmother's house. The only home he'd ever known.

Flinging himself into the truck cab, he cranked the key in the ignition. He threw the truck in Reverse. The tires spun gravel as he jolted onto the paved road.

He shouldn't have come over this afternoon. He'd come against his better judgment. Against his common sense.

Breaking his vow. Using Gray as an excuse. Because he hadn't been able to stomach another minute without seeing Gray's mother.

Getting involved with the Montgomerys had been an

error in judgment. Somehow they'd penetrated his carefully erected barricade of self-protection.

A mistake from which—his stomach twisted—he feared
he might never recover.

Chapter Thirteen

The following Wednesday, while upstairs folding laundry, Kristina heard the screen door in the kitchen slam. She frowned but went back to folding the bath towel, warm from the dryer. But at the sound of glass breaking, she ran out of the bedroom.

"Gray?" She dashed downstairs. "Is that you?"

Water dribbled off the kitchen island. Against the floorboard, one of her glass vases lay splintered into shards. Fortunately, a cheap vase from a discount store. Not one of her mother's.

Gray leaned over the sink. His hands gripped the edge of the counter. The muscles in his shoulder blades knotted.

"Honey, are you hurt? What happened? I thought you were over at Canyon's—"

"I was over at Canyon's, all right."

Stepping over the broken glass, she touched his shoulder. "Tell me what's wrong. Maybe I can help."

He whipped around, throwing off her hand. "You've helped enough."

Stung, she drew back. Glass crunched beneath her heels. "I don't know what you mean. What do you think I've done?"

His eyes blazed. "Why didn't you stop me from behaving like an idiot?"

"Gray—"

"Why didn't you tell me the truth? That a guy like me stood zero chance with a girl like her."

"Gray—"

"She's going to the dance with a stupid football jock!"

Kristina remembered the boy from the pancake supper. "Oh, I'm so sorry. I had no—"

"You went shopping with her for a dress, and what? It didn't come up? That she already had a date for the dance?"

"Gray, sweetheart—"

"I thought she was better than that."

"When we went shopping, Jade didn't have a date."

The defiance drained from Gray in a whoosh. He slumped against the counter. "She said she wasn't the kind of girl to sit around waiting for life to happen."

"Jade told me she wanted to go to the dance with you."

His mouth turned down. "Everybody at school knows what it means to go to a dance with one of those lunkheads. And he's a senior."

"That doesn't sound like our Jade."

"News flash, Mom. She's made it clear she's not *our* Jade." He pushed out his lower lip. "Or at least, most definitely not my Jade."

"I hoped she'd wait for you to ask her."

He frowned. "Like mother, like son, she said. What did she mean by that, Mom?"

Kristina's chest tightened.

"I wasn't playing games, Mom, I promise. I was working up the courage to ask her."

Kristina braved one more attempt to place her arm around her son's shoulders. This time, he let her. "I know, honey."

His chocolate eyes melted her heart. "I'm not that sort of guy. Real men don't play games with people's hearts. Dad wouldn't. Uncle Weston wouldn't. Canyon wouldn't, either."

No, Canyon wouldn't. If anyone was playing games with someone's heart, it was Kristina.

"I really like her." Gray's eyes moistened. "Just the way she is. And I thought she liked me, too." He averted his gaze. "Stupid, huh?"

She hugged him. "You are a great catch, Grayson Montgomery."

He grimaced. "Is this one of those 'any girl would be lucky to have you as her date' speeches?"

Kristina's lips quirked. "As a matter of fact, it is."

He let out an exaggerated sigh. But the moisture had disappeared from his eyes. "I'm sorry about the vase. I came busting in, and my elbow accidentally caught it. I'll clean up the mess."

She suppressed a sigh of relief. Gray had never been prone to temper tantrums as a child, and she was glad that, when life didn't go his way, he still wasn't.

"I love you, son."

He wrested a broom out of the pantry. "You might be the only one."

She sighed. "But now I'm not sure what to do. I told the dance committee I'd help chaperone after the Good Friday service at church."

He swept the glass fragments into the bin.

"You would've looked so handsome in your suit, too…"

His head shot up. "Oh, you'll see me. The more the merrier. I'm going to keep watch over Jade and that over-privileged bag of testosterone, whether she likes it or not."

She reached for the broom. "Careful. Don't cut yourself."

"You're such a mom, Mom."

She gave him a quick hug. "Just wait till it's your turn. Parenting is the toughest job you'll ever love."

Canyon wasn't proud of running away from Gray and Kristina. He'd done so only out of sheer self-preservation.

Sitting in a café booth overlooking the square with a potential client, he watched Kristina emerge from the church next door.

His pulse went into overdrive. And he spilled his coffee on the bill. The dark liquid streaked across the Formica table.

The tourism director—who needed aerial photos for a "Welcome to the Shore" video—hopped out of the booth. Grabbing a load of napkins from the dispenser, Canyon apologized profusely and frantically mopped up the mess he'd created.

Not unlike the mess in which he found himself with Kristina. His eyes cut to the window again, but Kristina was nowhere in sight. Just as well.

Canyon retrieved the sopping bill off the table, leaving the wad of wet napkins. "I've got this. Maybe we could talk more next week?"

The client moved toward the exit. "Maybe." The door jingled in his wake. And there went next month's groceries.

"Sorry," he murmured to Dixie behind the cash register. "I'm not usually such a klutz."

Dixie refused to take the soggy paper from him. "I won't be able to make head or tails of this thing, sugar. Tell me what it was you ordered again?"

"Two coffees. Two plates of Long Johns."

He extracted the bills from his wallet. She deposited the money and closed the tray with a bang.

Canyon jerked his thumb toward the booth. "It's wrecked, I'm afraid."

Dixie propped her elbows on the counter. "Like your heart these days?"

He blinked. "Uh…"

Dixie nudged her chin toward the window. "If you hurry, you can catch her. She spends a lot of time window gazing at the empty storefront down the block."

Canyon stared blankly at the fiftysomething peroxide blonde.

Dixie shooed him. "Don't stand there like an open-mouthed bass on a hook. Get out there and get your girl."

"Kristina's not— Wait..." He stuffed his hands in his pockets. "How do you—"

"Sugar." Dixie folded her arms across her bubblegum-pink waitress uniform. "Is this or is this not Kiptohanock? Stop stalling, Collier. I thought crop dusters were made of sterner stuff."

Pivoting, he made a hasty retreat.

Outside, he paused for a moment to get a bearing on Kristina. His gaze swept past the public dock and adjacent Coast Guard station to the soon-to-open turtle rehab center. He made it a point not to look at the gazebo.

His gaze traveled—almost against his will—to the slight rise of land at the western end of town. To the cemetery where his grandmother's remains rested. Hap Wallace's, too.

Near the fire station, he spotted Kristina lingering in front of what had been a hardware store in the village's heyday. Boarded over the entirety of his living memory, though.

He strode through the parking lot and across the church lawn. Crossing at the corner, he tossed a quick glance toward the gazebo as a songbird trilled.

So intent was her gaze through the taped-over display window, Kristina didn't hear his approach. Not wishing to startle her, he scuffled a few loose pebbles on the cracked sidewalk to warn her.

Kristina whirled. "Oh, it's you."

She placed her hand over her heart. Over the dog tags Canyon had learned to hate.

Not her husband. Or his memory. What Canyon hated

was the hold the past had on her present. He swallowed against a rush of feeling.

All those flying lessons. The exhilaration of soaring in the Cessna with Kristina. They'd once talked so freely. He hated the awkwardness between them. Awkward because of his feelings for her. Feelings she didn't return.

He shouldn't have followed her here. He turned to go.

"Wait—"

He stopped.

She cleared her throat. "How are Jade's grades?"

"I think she's turned the corner, academically. Socially?" He shrugged. "Still trying to find her place in high school. Still circling for a safe place to land."

"Aren't we all?" Kristina tilted her head. "Sometimes I think we spend our lives trying to find a safe place to land."

"Amen," he muttered.

She laughed, the sound like tinkling bells. And the tension between them dissolved.

"Are you doing okay, Canyon?"

His heart sped up a notch. "As well as could be expected." He fought past his own fears. "Since I don't get to see you every day."

She blushed. But her hand didn't stray to that hateful chain around her neck. A small victory, but he'd take what he could get.

"You come here often, I hear."

Her eyes darted to his. "Someone's been spreading tales."

"There are no secrets in Kiptohanock, remember?" He pressed his nose to the glass. "Make a nice florist shop, wouldn't it?"

She exhaled. "How is it you know me so well?"

"Not as well as I'd like."

A blush crept up the collar of her wraparound dress. But she didn't move away.

"You're mighty dressed up for a Thursday."

The blue dress tied at her narrow waist. His mouth went dry at the ache to feel her in his arms again.

"I went to see a Realtor."

He smiled. "The first step is always the hardest. But I'm proud of you."

She rocked on her heels. "I didn't say I was going to put in a bid."

"The owner would probably give you a deal to take the place off his hands."

Her eyes dropped to the pavement. "The price was very fair."

Canyon crossed his arms across his chest. "I'd be glad to loan you the start-up money."

She shook her head. "Why would you do that? You're not exactly rolling in the dough. You have to think about Jade's future, too."

He bristled. "I'm doing okay. Jade will be fine. A florist shop would be a good investment."

"You believe that much in the village?"

"I believe that much in you."

A vein jumped in the hollow of her throat. "I don't know what to say."

"I have faith in you and your dreams, Kristina. I'll always be on your side."

"Faith…" She squared her shoulders. "I appreciate your offer, more than you know. But Pax left me enough so that money isn't the issue."

"What is the issue then, Kristina?"

"Suppose I try and fail?"

"We've had this conversation before. Suppose you try and succeed? But maybe that's the real problem. If you succeed, it means you've moved into a new life, and that thought scares you to death."

"There's Gray to consider." She lifted her chin. "I can't neglect my son."

"Gray would make a great delivery boy." Canyon smirked. "When he's not working at my airfield."

She threw out her arms. "You've got this whole thing figured out, don't you?"

"I don't have you figured out at all, Kristina. But you need to trust yourself and what you feel. Don't listen to the fear."

She glanced behind him in the direction of the songbird. "I stopped dreaming a long time ago, Canyon."

"I don't believe that." He motioned toward the darkened store. "What do you see when you look through the glass? Dream with me, Kristina. Allow yourself for once to just dream with me."

She stared at him. "Van Cortlandt blue."

"Excuse me?"

"That's what I see when I look through the window." She fluttered her hand. "It's a paint color, flyboy."

He bit back a smile. "What else do you see?"

"I see that fabulous antique counter and those wide-planked floors sanded and returned to their original luster." She slumped. "I also see it would require an enormous amount of work—not to mention expense—to renovate the space."

He fingered his chin. "Which is why you have me and teenagers." He dropped his hand and smiled. "Slave labor."

She peered in the window again. "I wondered if, maybe when Sawyer's done with the aquatic center, he might give me a reasonable price on the remodel."

"Good idea. What else?"

Stretching, she gestured against the glass. "See those shelves?"

He squinted through the smudged plate glass. "Uh-huh…"

"Perfect for merchandise." She framed her vision, her hands bracketing an L. "And this wonderful front window? Seasonal displays. Like when winter turns into spring."

"Sounds like a plan." He caught her hand. "And a song. In fact, I think I hear a nightingale."

Humming a few bars of "A Nightingale Sang in Berkeley Square," Canyon placed her hands on his chest and held them there.

Kristina's gaze darted left and right. "What are you doing?"

Not giving her time to resist, he swung her around on the sidewalk. "I'm finishing our dance."

"I don't want to dance." She tried pulling her hands free. "Someone is going to see us, Canyon."

He swayed to the right and then to the left. "Colliers learned a long time ago not to live their lives caring what other people think."

She huffed but relaxed, splaying her fingers against the fabric of his shirt.

"Close your eyes and dream." Drawing her closer, he encircled her waist with his hands. "Dance with me, Kristina," he whispered against her ear.

With a small sigh, her body began to move with his as they danced.

Around and around they danced in front of the storefront that begged for her to bring it to life. As she'd brought him to life. Dancing to music only they could hear. Together.

His lips brushed against the silky strands of her hair. "You make this pilot want to sing."

She bit her lip. "You make me want to dream. To feel again. Like winter has finally turned into spring."

"With you, it feels like spring to me, Kris."

A sea breeze lifted the hair on his forehead. She feathered the curl off his brow. He flushed at the touch of her hand.

Her hand moved to cup his jaw. "I had no idea you could be so romantic."

"Me neither."

Placing her hands around his face, she kissed him.

"I love you, Kristina."

Eyes widening, she wrenched free. She fell against the rough brick of the abandoned building. Without her in his arms, he felt bereft.

Her chest heaved. "I've only said those words to one man. I can't say them again, Canyon, unless I'm sure I mean them with my whole heart."

Canyon knew, even if she didn't, she couldn't have kissed him like that unless somewhere in her heart, she already did love him.

"If you tell me there's a chance you could love me one day—no matter how long it takes—I'll wait. You're worth waiting for, Kristina." His heart jackhammered.

Her china-blue eyes shimmered with unshed tears. "I can't make you any promises, Canyon. I can't ask you to wait."

"You're not asking. I'm offering." He reached for her. "I'll be your safe landing, Kristina, if you'll let me."

She shied at his outstretched hand. "I'm trying to let go of the past. I can't say when I'll be ready." She took his hand, weaving her fingers in his. "But wait for me, Canyon. Please don't give up on me."

He drew her into his arms again. His heart slowed to a steadier beat. "Take as much time as you need. As long as I know at the end of the day, you'll be there waiting for me."

Kristina took a shuddery breath. "This is scarier than flying."

"Sweeter, too," he rasped.

Kristina smiled.

"And I won't ever give up on us, Kris." He swallowed. "I couldn't even if I tried."

Chapter Fourteen

When Canyon agreed to let Jade go to the dance—and spent a chunk of change on a new dress—he'd assumed she'd go with Gray.

Now Canyon realized the runway to perdition was paved with false assumptions. He wouldn't make that mistake again.

His first instinct had been to lock Jade in her room until she turned thirty. His next move? Consult someone who'd been in the same predicament in which he found himself.

Therefore, he sought out the best adviser on daughters he knew—Seth Duer, Sawyer's father-in-law—for an emergency chat at the Sandpiper Café over a plate of Long Johns.

Seth's mustache quirked at hearing Canyon's solution. "You realize the sheer physical impossibility—not to mention the legality—of trying to keep Jade under lock and key till she's thirty, don't you?"

Canyon scrubbed his neck with his hand. "If this is a taste of the future, I'm not going to survive this adolescent roller coaster."

Seth's bushy eyebrows bunched. "What you need are high expectations, boundaries and a whole lot of prayer."

"Oh, believe me when I tell you there's a whole lot of prayer going on these days." He gripped the white porcelain mug. "About a whole lot of things."

Seth smiled, but then the gravelly voiced waterman's

blue-green eyes turned sad. "A lesson I learned too late for my oldest, Lindi. But it doesn't have to be that way with your niece."

Lindi went looking for love in the wrong places. And when Lindi died, her younger sister, Amelia, was left to raise Lindi's infant son, Max. Canyon couldn't afford to make the same mistake with Jade.

As long as he had breath in his body, he couldn't—wouldn't—allow Jade to destroy her life. History didn't have to repeat itself in terms of Beech and Brandi. The Collier curse had to end—with Jade.

He also gave Margaret Davenport a call, seeking a female perspective.

"Give Jade a little leeway. She needs to prove she's worthy of the trust you're placing in her. Make it a short rope, though." Margaret's tone sharpened. "Just enough rope for that jock to hang himself if he gets out of hand with our girl."

The learning curve was steep and fast in what he was realizing might be the most important job he'd ever have—fathering Jade. On-the-job training at its scariest. And finest.

A sheen of sweat broke out on his forehead when he broached the topic with Jade. He had a serious—and awkward—talk with her on what he expected and what he wouldn't tolerate. Naturally, Jade was incensed.

"You don't trust me," she shouted.

"I don't trust seventeen-year-old boys," he countered. "And I intend to fight for your future whether you fight for yourself or not."

"You ought to take a good look in the mirror, take a short walk through the woods—" she pointed in the general direction of Kristina's house "—and practice what you preach."

"Don't try to change the subject." He scowled. "You, this boy and the dance are not negotiable."

She stomped to her bedroom. "I hate you." And slammed the door in his face.

"I guess this means you won't be naming any children after me then?" he yelled.

Something thudded against the panel. He jumped back just to be safe. But it was time to be the dad he'd never had. Whether Jade liked it or not.

On the night of the school dance, he pushed aside the curtain as a flashy convertible rolled into the airfield. The car idled for a second and then the driver laid on the horn.

"Why didn't you tell me he was here?" Hurrying into the living room, Jade reached for the door handle.

Canyon placed his palm firmly against the door. "Not so fast."

She gave Canyon a haughty look. "He's waiting for me."

Canyon gave her a cool look of his own. "He can continue to wait unless he comes inside like a real man and introduces himself to me. We're going to have a chat."

Her mouth flattened. "Why are you being so difficult?"

Canyon's eyebrows rose. "You haven't seen difficult until I've checked out the boy taking my girl out in his car."

Her eyes rolled. "You're going to make us late for the dance."

Blocking the door, he rested his shoulder against the frame. "Not moving." He cocked his head. "Got all night. How 'bout you?"

Jade let out a shriek. "You're being impossible."

Canyon smiled. "You haven't seen impossible, darlin', if I decide that boy isn't good enough for you."

Her mouth fell open. "He's a senior."

"Exactly." Canyon glared. "I wasn't born yesterday. Once upon a time, I was him."

"This is ridiculous…" she sputtered.

But straightening, he swung open the door and motioned to the boy in the car. "His choice."

He met the boy on the stoop. At first glance, he took a dislike to the boy and his slicked-back pompadour. Since when had that hairstyle made a comeback? But most of all, he took issue with the way the boy eyed Jade—like he was sizing up a piece of beef.

Or maybe that was Canyon projecting his own fears. Protectiveness and pride rose in equal measure.

Jade looked amazing in her soft green dress. The flared hem brushed her kneecaps. The magenta streak in her hair had faded some. And she'd used a light hand on the makeup tonight. Her eyes no longer resembled a raccoon's.

Who was this girl and what had she done with Jade? He didn't like Jade feeling she had to change her identity to be accepted. At least the eyebrow ring and multiple ear studs were still in place or he would've despaired entirely.

He stuck out his hand to the boy. "Canyon Collier. Jade's uncle."

The boy took his hand. "Harrison Randolph." He smirked. "Her date."

Canyon squeezed the boy's hand until Randolph winced from the pressure. "Jade has her phone. I expect her home by midnight."

Jade's pink lips—where had his goth girl gone?—thinned. "That's not fair."

The boy went rigid. "The dance doesn't end—"

"I also think you ought to know I've had training in weaponry," Canyon said. "You roger that, Randolph?"

Uncertainty flickered in the boy's gaze. "Loud and clear."

Canyon jabbed his index finger at the boy's starched tuxedo shirt. "That would be sir to you." He whipped around to Jade. "And you will call me on the hour, every hour, with a status report."

With a short jerk of his head, the boy nodded.

Why hadn't Canyon thought to teach Jade a few self-defense strategies? He watched the red taillights of the expensive convertible disappear into the darkness. Proud of how lovely and grown-up Jade looked. Worried sick at how lovely and grown-up Jade looked.

He paced the hallway. He ought to plug this month's data into his office computer. But he couldn't concentrate.

Restless, he decided to tackle sorting through the musty old cardboard box Margaret had given him at his grandmother's funeral three years ago. A task he'd never had the time or courage to face before. But tonight, he suspected, was going to be all about courage.

One yellowed black-and-white photo in particular captured his attention. His teenage grandmother stood on the church steps between two young men in World War II–era uniforms. On the back of the photograph his grandmother had written in a fluid hand—back when they taught handwriting in school—"Easter Sunrise Service, 1945."

He flipped the picture to study his grandmother's face. So young. So beautiful. Her eyes clear. Totally unaware of the blows life would deal her.

The young man on the right to whom she'd give everything—his grandfather, Freddie Collier—would leave her and their baby girl for the lure of adventure. Hap Wallace—on her left—would give her his heart and lifelong devotion. She'd return the favor by never loving him back.

Jade looked so much like his grandmother, Canyon rose abruptly from the kitchen table. He drifted into the living room. After thirty minutes of not listening to a documentary, he turned off the television and resumed his pacing. This parenting gig wasn't for cowards.

Canyon wished he could talk the situation over with Kristina. Her practical common sense made him feel better. Once he'd found out Jade wasn't going to the dance with Gray, the only reason he'd allowed her to go was that Kristina had told him she'd be chaperoning.

He'd flown in hurricanes and participated in hundreds of rescues in the Coast Guard, but nothing came close to the gnawing fear inside him. If something happened to Jade...

Canyon drew a quick breath. He'd never forgive himself. This love he felt for Jade had ambushed him out of nowhere and continued to surprise him, only deepening with time.

As for Kristina? Was he giving her too much leeway? Would she ever move beyond the past? Maybe despite his promise to wait, in the end he'd be the one swinging high and dry from a rope.

Was there such a thing as too much patience? Was his reluctance to not force the issue based more on his fears of rejection? Or a desire to delay what he secretly feared was inevitable? That she'd never love him the way he loved her.

Perhaps Jade was right. Maybe it was time he fought for Kristina, for what they could be together, for their future. Even if Kristina couldn't see she needed to fight for herself.

Kristina searched the girls' restroom stalls for the fifth time. Same result. She sagged against the tiled wall.

No sign of Jade. Outside the girls' bathroom, music boomed from the gymnasium dance floor. The beat of the bass vibrated through the wall and thrummed against her temples.

One job. She'd had one job—to make sure no harm came to Jade—and she'd failed. Canyon would never forgive her if anything happened to his niece.

There could be no putting off the inevitable. She might be a coward about her own future, but she wouldn't allow Jade's life to be in jeopardy.

Covering one ear to block the pounding music, she cupped her cell phone to her other ear. He picked up on the first ring.

"I can't find Jade."

"Krist—"

"Mrs. Montgomery?" Someone banged on the door. "Mrs. Montgomery, are you in there?"

"Hold on, Canyon." Removing the phone from her ear, she swung open the door and flinched as the music hit her in a wave of sound.

One of Gray's chess club friends hovered outside. "Gray wanted me to tell you he's sticking with Jade."

Why hadn't Gray come to her? But of course he hadn't. He didn't see himself as needing his mother. The same hero complex that eventually took his father's life.

Remembering she'd left Canyon hanging, she shouted into the phone. "Gray's gone, too. He's following Jade and her date wherever it is they've gone."

There were dire threats of imminent dismemberment on the other end of the line. "When I get my hands on that punk Randolph, I'm going to…"

She held the phone away from her ear.

Gray's friend Vincent cast a furtive look over his shoulder before leaning closer. "You didn't hear it from me, Mrs. Montgomery, but I overheard Randolph bragging about taking Jade for a moonlight ride on the water."

"On the water? What're you talking about?"

The pimple-faced boy frowned. "His dad docks a boat at a slip in Kiptohanock. Randolph wants to start his own party."

"Did you catch that, Canyon?" she bellowed into the phone, trying to be heard over the pulse-pounding beat.

He growled. And she had a sudden sympathy for the boy when Canyon got his hands on him.

"Don't do anything rash, Canyon."

"Oh, it won't be rash. By the time I get over to the marina, I'll have worked out a plan to tar and feather—"

She resisted the urge to laugh. "I'm heading there now. Wait for me."

"Uh, Mrs. Montgomery…" Vincent tugged on her sleeve. "Gray took your car."

"But Gray's only fifteen. He can't drive."

Vincent shrugged.

"I'll swing by the high school and pick you up," Canyon promised. "See you in ten."

But she'd no sooner punched Off than her cell buzzed again. Without stopping to check caller ID, she clicked On, supposing he'd forgotten to tell her something.

"I'll wait for you outside the—"

"Mom? Mom?"

Gray's raspy whisper startled Kristina. Nodding her thanks to Vincent, she dashed toward the exit.

She clutched the phone to her ear. "Are you all right?"

"Mom, there's no time. You've got to listen to me. Helmet Head is untying the mooring lines from the dock. He's taking the boat and Jade out on the water."

She stopped midstride on the sidewalk. "Canyon is picking me up. We'll head to the marina." She was getting a bad feeling about the whole situation. "Where are you, honey?"

A protracted sigh from her offspring. Over the phone, a motor cranked.

"He's going to be too late to help, Mom."

Kristina's stomach muscles tightened. "Gray? What have you done?"

"I'm not going to have cell service long, Mom. I can't let him hurt Jade. He's drinking. I know Jade's scared, and she's trapped on the boat. I won't let anything happen to her."

"Gray, where are you?"

"I'm going to jump on board at the last minute. He hasn't seen me yet. He's so drunk, if he wasn't hanging on to the wheel, he couldn't stand upright."

"Gray, I want you to wait for us—"

Sounds of an altercation.

"Gray, answer me. Gray…"

The connection went dead. And her heart went cold.

Chapter Fifteen

Canyon was only a minute from the high school when Kristina called again. Her voice was thready with panic as she relayed the latest update.

"The football player is twice Gray's size. He'll pulverize my son."

Canyon palmed the wheel as he turned onto the school campus. "We'll find them. Don't worry." He clicked off as he pulled alongside the curb where Kristina waited.

She tossed her phone into her purse and scrambled into the Jeep. "Don't tell me not to worry. He's my son."

Laying his phone on the console, Canyon steered out of the parking lot and onto the highway. "Jade's not answering her phone, either. There's no cell service out in the inlet. Let's not assume the worst."

Her beautiful blue eyes went stormy. "What could be worse than our children on the open water with an out-of-control teenager at the helm?" She grabbed hold of the dashboard as he took the curve at heightened speed.

"Buckle up, Kris. It's going to be a bumpy ride." He rattled over the small Quinby bridge.

"You worry about finding our kids. Let me worry about me." But bouncing, she hit the roof. "Ouch!"

"Seat belt, Kristina," he growled.

"What was I thinking?" Lines creased her forehead. "I

can't open a florist shop. My job is to be Gray's mother first and foremost. This disaster is all my fault."

His gut tightened. Always putting herself and any hope of a future last.

"This is not your fault, Kristina. If anyone is to blame, it's me. I should've trusted my instincts and never let Jade out the door with Randolph."

"If anything happens to my son—" her voice quavered "—I'll never forgive myself."

"Gray can handle himself, Kristina. Teenagers make poor choices. That's the way they learn."

She glared at him. "That's assuming they aren't beaten to a pulp and live to make other choices."

"Have a little faith in your son, Kristina."

She flinched as if he'd hit a nerve.

"Gray's a good, smart kid. Besides, haven't you ever listened to airline safety instructions?"

Her eyes narrowed. "What has that got to do with anything?"

"Flight attendants instruct parents to put their oxygen mask on first before attempting to help their children."

"Your point?"

"It's not about being selfish. It's common sense." He gripped the wheel so tightly his knuckles whitened. "If you don't take care of your need for air first, you won't have the oxygen to give anyone else the help they require."

She throttled the seat belt strap. "So you're telling me to breathe?"

"I'm also telling you to buckle your seat belt."

She clicked the seat belt across her chest. "There. Satisfied?"

He clenched his jaw as he veered past the road to Wachapreague. "When it comes to you, Kristina, not by a long shot. You can't avoid the feelings between us."

A vein pulsed in her delicate throat. "I thought avoidance was your thing."

"I'd hoped after the other day on the sidewalk, we'd moved past this."

She lifted her chin. "I've never denied we have chemistry."

He fought to control the wheel and his temper. "You don't kiss someone like you kissed me, Kristina, and expect me to believe you don't feel something for me."

She shook her head. "I can't talk about this with you. Not now."

"Then when?" He veered past the road to Wachapreague. "Maybe I'm wrong. Maybe you've already put on your oxygen mask. Maybe you just need to be brave enough to take the first whiff of air."

Shaking, she balled her hands in her lap. He should've known better than to get into it with her. Neither one of them could think straight with the kids in danger.

Entering Kiptohanock, he careened around the village square. With a screech of brakes, he rolled into an empty space in front of the small Coast Guard station. Thrusting open the Jeep door, he staggered out.

Her Subaru sat in the deserted café parking lot, adjacent to the town pier. As did the flashy convertible.

It didn't take long to get Seth Duer's son-in-law Braeden Scott—the Officer in Charge—up to speed.

Braeden sighed. "You know how many creeks and barrier islands dot the coast. I'll send out the patrol boat, but without GPS coordinates, it could take a while to locate them."

Kristina bit her lip.

Braeden touched her shoulder. "Best thing for you to do is to go home. I'll call you the moment I have any news, I promise." He darted a meaningful look at Canyon. "Take care of each other."

Canyon hated the helpless feeling. One look at Kristina's face, and he knew she felt the same. Her hands shook as she rummaged through her purse for her keys.

He spotted the keys through the window of her car and opened the unlocked door. "Gray left the keys in the ignition."

Chewing her lip, she slipped behind the wheel. Under any other circumstances, he would've told her how beautiful she looked in her lacy black dress. She didn't look like the mother of a teenage son.

With her hair wavy and hanging to her shoulders, his old friend Hap Wallace would've said she possessed a soft beauty. Like a misty soft morning over the tidal marsh. But her face was strained. And the worry in her eyes probably reflected his own.

She stared over the harbor as if she could spot one tiny boat amid the darkness of the night. Her hands gripped the steering wheel in a stranglehold of frustration. The same frustration he felt.

Jade should've called him the minute Randolph wanted to leave the dance. What was she thinking, going out on the water with that jerk?

When Canyon got hold of her, he was going to…hug the daylights out of her. And then he'd lock her in her room until she turned thirty.

"There is one other thing we should do, Kris."

"I'm open to any ideas," she whispered.

"We should pray."

"You're right. In the old days, prayer was my go-to." Breath trickled from between her lips. "You're a good influence on me, Canyon."

He laughed. "That's one for the record books. I've never been called a good influence before. Why don't I follow you home?"

"Thank you. For being here for Gray. And for me."

If only she'd allow him to show her how much he wanted to always be there for her. Every day. In every situation of life. But now was not the time.

He retraced his steps to the Jeep. The time never seemed to be right for them. He had a sinking fear that somehow the timing would never be right.

Midnight had come and gone. He kept her taillights in sight until she turned into her driveway. He also kept up a running prayer for God to watch over Jade, Gray and even the Randolph boy.

It was incredibly humbling that the God of the universe listened to someone like Canyon. Though Reverend Parks had been quick to assure him it was true. That each and every time he prayed, God was eager to hear from His beloved, if wayward, child.

Not unlike how he'd be glad to hear Jade's voice. Though knowing Jade, her voice would probably include a great deal of sarcasm and attitude.

He'd only been home about fifteen minutes when he heard a knock at the door. Surely Braeden would've called unless… His blood roared in his ears.

Bad news was always delivered in person. His heart in his throat, he lunged for the door. But it wasn't what he expected.

It took his heart a moment to settle. Not a Coastie. Kristina.

She'd changed out of her dress into jeans and a long-sleeved gray T-shirt. She'd scraped her hair into a messy ponytail at the nape of her neck. "Mind if I wait with you?"

He'd wanted to be with her, but she hadn't invited him to stop at her place. And with their emotions running high, he hadn't wanted to push her any farther.

Kristina's eyes watered. "I couldn't stand being alone."

Him, either. "So you dashed over without a coat."

That earned a smile. "Story of my life."

He ushered her inside out of the chill. "Let me get you something warm." He lumbered toward his bedroom and searched his closet for something clean. He pulled out a blue-striped plaid shirt.

Canyon returned to the living room to find Kristina huddled on his leather sofa. "Put this on."

She shrugged into the oversize shirt. It went without saying she looked way better in his shirt than he ever had. Shivering, she tucked her hands underneath her arms.

He started for the hall closet. "I can get you my coat, too."

"No." She swallowed. "I'll be better once we pray." She laid her upturned palm on the seat.

He sank onto the cushion next to her. He leaned forward, placing his knotted hands on his knees.

"Remember, I'm rusty at this," she joked in a husky voice.

But she closed her eyes and whispered an entreaty for God to bring their children home. He began praying where Kristina left off.

His prayer was wobbly at first, but gradually the desperation and fear receded. To be replaced with a weird and—based on outward appearances—totally unjustified sense of calm.

From time to time, both fell silent. Comfortable stretches of silence. At one point during the endless night, he made a pot of coffee. He grabbed clean mugs from the cabinet and poured two cups.

She backed away. "I don't need—"

"Fully loaded with cream and sugar, it's good for shock. You might not need it, but I do. Don't make me drink alone."

She accepted the cup and took a sip. Reading the outside of the mug, her mouth curved. "Oh, really? Good to know."

"What?"

She turned the mug so he could read the print.

Helicopter Pilots Are Cuter.

Canyon rolled his eyes. "Jade signed for the UPS package last week. Apparently, the delivery included more than office supplies."

Kristina pointed at the cup in his hand. "I like your cup, too."

He gave the cup a half turn.

I Can't Help Being Awesome—I'm a Helicopter Pilot.

Kristina laughed so hard she had to put down her mug. "I love that girl of yours."

"Right back at you with Gray."

She twined her hand in his. "It'll be light soon. I'd like to pray again, if that's all right?"

It was more than all right. He wouldn't have believed it possible until tonight. But praying with Kristina had been like a soothing salve over the scabbed but never healed places in his heart.

Sitting down, he bowed his head, all nervousness, doubt and self-consciousness gone. His voice deepened, and Kristina scooted closer until the side of her knee touched his.

He stopped to take a breath. When the landline phone rang, he jumped up, Kristina at his elbow.

Trying to absorb the information from Braeden, he made a frantic search on the cluttered coffee table for a pen and paper.

She sifted through the day's mail until she found a blank envelope and handed him a pencil.

"Could you repeat those coordinates?" He wrote furiously, listening for a few seconds.

"What?" she mouthed.

"Thank you so much, Braeden, for letting me know. I'll get the chopper in the air ASAP and stay in radio contact." He clicked off.

"What's happening, Canyon?"

She wasn't going to like this. He didn't like it, either. But now was not the time to go to pieces. He hoped as a former military wife, she was tougher than she looked.

"The station received a mayday from Randolph's boat."

Her eyes went large. "A distress call?"

"It was Jade. Something's wrong with the boat. It's taking on water."

Kristina steepled her hands under her chin. "What about Gray?"

"She didn't mention Gray, just that they were in trouble and needed help."

Kristina's fingers fumbled for the chain she wore around her neck. "The Guard has their coordinates. They'll get there—they have to get there in time."

He grabbed his jacket. "There was only the one distress call, Kris." He opened the door. "Radar lost contact. The signal simply vanished from the screen as if they'd never been there."

To her credit, she didn't fall apart. But her eyes became luminous. "What does that mean?"

He averted his gaze. "I think you know what that means."

She hung on to his arm. "I need to hear you say it. Please, Canyon. There's nothing worse than not knowing."

"Not knowing is what I've got. We know their last known location, but losing the signal most likely indicates the boat has submerged."

She trembled. "Which most likely means our children are in the water."

"Braeden has launched the rapid response boats. But—"

She tugged him toward the door. "But you could reach them faster in the chopper. What are we waiting for? Let's go."

"We?"

She widened her feet to hip's width. "You fly the helo, but you'll need a spotter."

"Are you sure? You've never been in the chopper before."

"You need me." Her eyes bored into him. "Don't you?"

He needed Kristina in more ways than she could ever understand—or probably handle at this moment. But she was right. In a search-and-rescue operation, time was of the essence. More eyes made for a better outcome.

"Okay," he conceded with reluctance. *Please, God, let this be a rescue and not a recovery of bodies.*

Truth was, he needed God more than he'd ever needed anyone. His splendid isolation was over for good.

Chapter Sixteen

First light broke over the horizon as they lifted off from the launch pad at the airfield. Beside him in the cockpit, Kristina latched on to the seat. But this was not the way she'd imagined enjoying a sunrise with Canyon.

He shot her a worried look. "Are you sure—"

"Go." She nudged her chin. "Just go."

She didn't miss the irony that her son's life—her very heartbeat—depended on another man's piloting skills. And on God's grace. Her faith since Pax's death had been woefully shaken on both counts.

Her anger—like subterranean lava beneath an outwardly dormant volcano—flared. Would God let her down again? Would she lose everyone she loved for good this time?

She ignored the urge to quiet her thoughts. To breathe. To trust.

Where had believing gotten her? At the age of thirty-eight, a widowed single parent. She was tired of being alone. Fighting alone. Living alone.

Then don't be alone.

Kristina turned toward Canyon. With a grim set to his mouth, he concentrated on clearing the trees. The chopper whizzed over the tin roof of her bungalow.

She fitted the headphones in place. "Where are we headed? And if you ask me one more time if I'm okay, I'm going to deck you."

He cut his eyes at her. "But who would fly the chopper?" His eyebrows rose. "You?"

"I might surprise you."

His features lightened for a second. "You never cease to amaze me, Kris."

She glanced away from the intensity of his gaze. From the warm hope in his eyes. "I wish I believed in myself as much as you believe in me."

"I wish you did, too."

She looked at him, but he'd redirected his focus onto following a set of coordinates. "Their last recorded location was beyond the Neck."

Kristina gasped as the chopper flew over the blue-green waters of the inlet. "Beyond Weston's lighthouse? That's open water."

Images flooded her mind of her son and Jade foundering as ocean waves broke over their heads— Her breath hitched.

He touched her arm. "Steady now, Montgomery."

She sucked in a deep breath.

"Braeden put in a call to the station at Chincoteague. The coordinates are about halfway between the two Coastie districts, but—"

"We're faster." She squared her shoulders. "And we're going to find them."

Canyon's eyes crinkled. "Yes, we are."

He maintained constant radio contact with the patrol units in the water. Zooming over the rocky lighthouse point, she bit back tears. No sign of them near land.

Canyon flew in a carefully plotted, ever-widening search pattern. She refused to dwell on the what-ifs. Worst-case scenario, there'd be plenty of time for regrets and recrimination. She couldn't—she wouldn't—lose Pax's son, too.

Her eyes strained to detect anything irregular in shape or color amid the rolling waves below. He flew as low as he dared. She fought the urge to draw up her feet as the chopper skimmed the air above the frothy waters of the ocean.

Despite a few false sightings, she quickly learned to distinguish between channel markers and people in the water.

Static crackled. He pressed the mic. "Roger that." Releasing the button, he angled. "Braeden's team has located the partially submerged boat."

Her pulse accelerated. "Did he find the children?"

More static. Canyon's face fell. "The boat has overturned. They've found a floating cooler." He swallowed. "And a life jacket."

She went rigid. "Oh, no. No. No."

"An empty life jacket." He covered her hand with his. "No bodies, though. Only debris. Braeden thinks the boat must've been traveling at a high rate of speed. Slamming down on the waves hard enough to break the seal."

She pounded her fist into her thigh. "Those stupid, stupid kids. Why do they always think they're immortal?"

Canyon banked left. She grabbed on to the seat.

"I flew this route with the migratory bird count last month. There's a barrier island nearby. Maybe they were able to swim there."

She clenched her teeth. "How near?"

The blades ate the air. A muscle ticked in his jaw. "Five miles."

"Five—" She crushed her knuckles against her mouth. "That's too far to swim, even if they knew there was an island out there. Which, in the dark, they probably didn't."

She wanted to weep. She wanted to scream. She wanted to jump out of the chopper and let the cold waters slide over her head forever.

As bad as the pain had been in losing her husband, this was far worse. She wasn't sure she'd survive losing a child.

"How long will they search?" Her voice rasped in the

mouthpiece. "How long before they declare it a recovery, not a rescue?"

"I won't stop looking, Kris."

She moaned. "I don't think I can do this again."

"We can't give up hope. As long as there's life, there's—"

"Don't say that to me." She threw out her hands. "Don't you get it? There is no life among the dead. Not for me. Not without Gray."

She pressed her face against the glass. What good was faith if she lost her son? Had Canyon been right? That when someone lost everything that was when faith meant the most.

Kristina rested her forehead against the chilly surface of the window. "Help me, God," she whispered.

She recalled those terrible days following the news of Pax's death. Her family, those dear sisters in arms, her church. The inexplicable peace. And she understood then that even when she lost Pax, she'd had God. She always had God. Her breath fogged the glass as she soaked in His peace.

Using the cuff of her sleeve, she wiped the window clean. And spotted something red winking below. In the tossing sea, a buoy swayed like a pendulum. The morning sun refracted off something else, too. She inched closer to get a better view. She inhaled sharply.

"There's someone clinging to the buoy." She pounded the window. "Canyon? Over there. Is it— Canyon, it's got to be them. Oh, God, please let it be them."

Doing a 180, Canyon brought the chopper around again and glimpsed the same metallic glitter Kristina had seen.

Her mouth trembled. "We've found them. We've found them."

Two figures crouched on the shallow rim of the buoy and clung to the steel girders of the channel marker.

His heart skipped a beat. Only two, but three souls had been missing.

From this distance, it was difficult to determine who'd survived. As he neared, the two buried their faces in their arms to ward off the spray churned by the rotors, further obscuring identification.

Drawing alongside, he hovered as close as he dared. Kristina frantically tugged at her seat belt.

He caught her hand. "I don't have the proper equipment to mount a rescue."

"We have to do something." She glared at him. "You have to do something. They've been out there all night. How much longer can they hold on?"

Something of which he was all too aware. Jade had left the house wearing ridiculously spiky heels and a filmy dress. She would've been in a far worse position to withstand the elements than the boys. Why hadn't he made sure she could swim?

Canyon radioed the Coast Guard station. After a short conversation, he backed off a few yards, holding the chopper as steady as the wind allowed.

"The response boat is only a few minutes out. We'll hang around until they arrive." He took Kristina's hand. "They're going to make it."

She squeezed his fingers. "But who didn't make it?"

He had no answers for her. The minutes ticked by. Agonizing minutes until he beheld the orange-and-white flag of the Coastie boat.

Keeping his distance, he watched the crew extract one of the kids from the buoy onto the response boat.

"That's Gray's jacket," Kristina shrieked.

Wind buffeted the chopper. Canyon surveyed the worsening conditions. A squall loomed on the horizon.

"There's someone else on a stretcher," Kristina called, riveted to the window. "Gray must've been shielding—"

"Green dress?" He thought his heart might explode.

"No…it's a dark coat." Her voice broke. "Oh, Canyon. I'm so sorry."

He took a ragged breath. Randolph had worn a dark tuxedo. The missing teen was Jade. *Oh, God. Please, no.*

A beeping sounded from the instrument panel. He leaned forward.

Kristina's gaze darted from the flashing red light to him. "What's wrong?"

He clamped his jaw. "We're going to have to refuel."

"Why is the boat leaving, Canyon?"

Dread twisted his belly. "Operation complete, they're headed to Kiptohanock. An emergency crew will be waiting to transport the survivors to Riverside Hospital."

The radio squawked. His hand shook as he reached for the mic to receive the incoming transmission. "Collier here. Report?"

He braced himself.

Canyon's breath left him in a whoosh of air. "Three?" His voice cracked. "Say again." His gaze darted to Kristina.

"Roger that." He released the button. "Three, Kristina. Dispatch says there are three alive and headed for port." He gripped the stick.

She collapsed into the seat. "Thank You, thank You, God. Whoa—" She grabbed the seat belt strap as the chopper banked a hard right. "What are you doing?"

"I'm headed for Kiptohanock."

"But what about your fuel tank?"

"Enough to get to town. I'm going to get my girl if I have to land this bird on the square with just fumes."

Which was exactly what he did.

The sound of the whirring blades brought the breakfast crowd out of the Sandpiper. On the marina dock, seasoned watermen ducked their heads as dust swirled.

With the rotors still spinning, he switched off the engine and threw himself out of the chopper. He'd taken two steps toward the Coast Guard station when he remembered Kristina.

In one smooth motion, he wheeled and threw open the passenger door. Shaking, her hands fumbled with the seat belt.

"Let me."

He lifted her from the helicopter. But on solid ground once more, she swayed. So he swung her into his arms and carried her across the green.

In a rapid stride, he clomped across the wooden planks of the dock. Sirens sounded behind them as an ambulance rounded the square. Followed by another one. They'd beaten the fast boat.

He made sure she'd regained her footing before he set her down this time. Together, they watched the response boat navigate the vessels bobbing in the harbor.

A crowd had formed along the seawall. Her hands clasped, she leaned into him. He wasn't sure he'd breathe properly again until he saw Jade with his own eyes.

The response boat eased alongside the Coastie pier. A seaman jumped across the gap, landing nimbly. Another Coastie threw him a line.

EMTs brushed the bystanders aside. Never had he wished he was still part of the Coastie team more than he did now. The uncertainty was killing him.

A couple of EMTs emerged from the vessel bearing a stretcher. Kristina strained forward. He took hold of her arm, preventing her from toppling face-first into the harbor. But the figure on the stretcher proved to be the Randolph boy.

One of the EMTs holding the stretcher inched by them. "He's battered and bruised but seems okay. Your girl will be out next, Collier."

Surprised, he nodded his thanks. He recognized the guy from his long-ago high school days.

The former wrestling star grinned. "I figured she had to belong to you. She's raising cain to get off the boat." He readjusted his hold on the stretcher. "Good to have you home again, Collier."

As the stretcher went past, a lithe figure clad in a suit coat much too large stepped onto the dock. Her windblown hair had dried sufficiently for the magenta strands to gleam in the sunlight.

Somewhere in the deep blue sea, she'd lost her shoes. But sunlight glinted off the multiple ear studs.

His mouth working, he sent up a silent prayer of gratitude that Jade hadn't entirely abandoned her goth girl ways. The metal studs had alerted Kristina to their location in the water. And saved their lives.

Mascara streaked Jade's cheeks. Her eyes seemed the largest thing in her too-pale face. A more pitiful sight he'd never seen. But she'd never looked more wonderful to him.

He raised his arm. "Jade!" He'd only taken two steps before she flung off the coat and ran toward him. Straight into his outstretched arms.

"Daddy!"

Had she just—He shook from head to toe. He'd been called a lot of names over the years—worthless, Coastie, pilot, neighbor. But none had ever sounded as sweet, right and true.

Canyon enfolded her into his embrace. "Hey, kid." Her skin felt so icy.

Sobs racked her frame. "I'm so sorry for everything."

His tough, never-say-die Jade. She clung to him as hard as she must've clung to the buoy.

Canyon cupped his hand over the top of her head as she buried her face into the fabric of his shirt. "I thought I'd lost you, baby," he whispered into her hair.

"I knew you'd come," came her fierce response. "I told them you'd find us. That you wouldn't stop looking." She gripped the lapels of his jacket in her fists.

He didn't know whether to laugh or to cry. So he did both. Kristina threw her arms around them, murmuring the nonsensical things women say to small children.

But when Gray called her name, she rushed to her son. Coatless and in his shirtsleeves, Gray staggered off the boat.

An EMT approached Canyon, a blanket in hand. "Your niece is hypothermic. She needs to go to the hospital."

Jade stiffened. "I want to stay with you."

His hands grasping her shoulders, he pulled back a few inches. "I'll be there, too. Always." He glanced around. "If someone will give me a ride."

Stepping out of the crowd, Seth Duer pointed his thumb to his old Silverado in the parking lot. Her arm around her shivering son, Kristina came alongside.

"You s-saved our lives, Canyon," Gray stuttered.

He shook his head. "Not me. Your mom spotted you. The Coasties saved you."

Kristina leaned her head on Gray's shoulder. "Without your chopper, I'm not sure the boat would've located them in time."

Gray's mouth quivered. "I don't know how much longer we could've held on."

Jade socked Canyon's shoulder. "You're a hero. Deal with it."

He smiled. There was the girl he knew. And loved.

But eager to change the subject, he took his first good breath. "What happened, Jade? Why did you get on the boat with that boy?"

She teared up again. "He said we would just stop by and see his dad's boat before he took me home. But when we got to the marina, he insisted I get on board to hear the engine."

Gray muttered something under his breath regarding jerks in football uniforms.

"I didn't know he'd stashed liquor on the boat." Her voice went little-girl small. "When he said our private party was just beginning, he scared me."

Canyon tensed. "Alcohol and boats do not mix."

"I told him I was getting off the boat and I'd walk home. But he threw off the lines and reversed out of the slip before I could stop him."

Gray straightened. "I knew she was in trouble. I knew I had to do something."

Jade threw Gray an admiring glance. "I didn't know Gray followed us. He jumped into the boat at the last minute."

Gray fingered his chin. "Helmet Head landed a lucky punch and knocked me down."

Kristina tried to examine his chin, but Gray batted her hand away.

Jade's brow puckered. "Harrison stumbled into the controls. The boat went into overdrive. We were going so fast. Too fast. The hull hit something."

Gray's shoulders rose and fell. "The next thing I knew, the boat was taking on water. Randolph was so out of it." He returned Jade's look of admiration. "She figured the radio couldn't be that different from the one at the airfield, so she called for help."

Jade shuddered. "And then we were in the water. There was no time to grab the life jackets. It took us both to keep Harrison afloat. Gray spotted the blinking channel marker, and we swam as hard as we could."

"You did everything right." Canyon cocked his head. "Other than going to the dance with an idiot boy and getting into a boat with him, that is." He kissed the top of her head. "But we'll discuss that later."

Jade managed a laugh. "Lesson learned. I was too concerned about looking cool and fitting in." She fingered her torn dress. "Not looking so cool now, though, am I?"

Canyon's heart quaked at the idea of her body lying at the bottom of the unyielding, dark ocean. During his stint in the Guard, he'd participated in the recovery of so many who, unlike Jade, hadn't made it.

Her face clouded. "The wind. The waves. We were so cold. I wasn't sure the transmission had gone through before the boat went down."

The EMTs started toward them. At Canyon's insistence, they loaded Gray into a vehicle first. Kristina, naturally, refused to be left behind.

He walked Jade to the second ambulance. "So you held fast to the buoy."

"Gray insisted I put on his coat to stay warm."

Canyon handed Jade up through the open ambulance doors. "I always knew I liked that boy."

An EMT seated Jade on a gurney beside the groaning Randolph and began taking her vitals. Canyon stepped into the van.

"We tried to keep Harrison out of the water and shared our body heat. All we could do was hold on." She grimaced. "Be seasick. And pray."

The EMT recorded her vitals on a clipboard. "We've gotta go."

Jade's green eyes widened. "Wait." She stretched out her hand. "Don't leave me."

"You're not getting rid of me that easily, kid." He took her frozen hand and warmed it with both of his. "Like it or lump it."

Her eyes misted. "I like it. A lot. I love you." Her lower lip wobbled. "Was it okay I called you Daddy?"

Canyon swallowed. "I love you, too, sweetheart. And being your daddy would be the best thing in the world to me."

She hugged him. His gaze watered.

He sniffed as he untangled her arms. "Those allergies."

She rolled her eyes. "You pilots."

"This pilot will be right behind the ambulance. And I'll stay in the ER with you until they let you come home."

"Home…" Jade whispered.

Canyon hopped down and reached to close the doors. "Home."

A word that could easily become his favorite word ever.

Chapter Seventeen

It was a long day keeping vigil while the doctors monitored Jade's condition. They had to wait for her official release papers before Canyon could take her home at last. He glanced at an incoming text on his cell from a hotshot firefighter buddy requesting Canyon's assistance with an out-of-control wildfire.

He'd call his friend and decline later. Right now, his priority was Jade. He powered down his phone. With her dress ruined, Canyon had promised to retrieve clean clothes from her bedroom so she could change out of her hospital gown and go home.

First, he decided to check on Gray. As for the other kid? Randolph had a hangover. And charges filed against him.

In the corridor, Canyon passed the boy's belligerent father, trying to justify his son's unjustifiable actions to Deputy Charlie Pruitt.

Canyon might be new to the whole parenting gig, but he'd learned one lesson early—children should face the consequences of their actions or history would repeat itself. Over and over again. And end up like his brother, Beech.

Pruitt signaled Canyon to wait. Closing his notepad, the deputy walked over to him. "I hear we have you to thank for rescuing the kids, Collier."

Canyon cut his eyes at the elder Randolph, yelling at his

attorney on a cell phone. "Not sure I did the world or the sheriff's department any favors with that one."

Pruitt's lip curled. "Overprivileged 'come here...'" He frowned and squared his shoulders. "I hope it goes without saying you didn't hear me say that out loud."

Feigning innocence, Canyon held both palms up. "Hear what?"

"Not a 'been here, 'born here like you and me, huh?" Pruitt pursed his mouth. "Not the Randolph kid's first time on our radar. Won't be the last. Some people seem drawn to trouble."

"And some of us don't have to go looking." Weary, Canyon leaned his shoulder against the wall. "Trouble seems to find us."

Pruitt cracked what Canyon supposed passed for a smile with law enforcement. "Not you. I figure that girl of yours is blessed to have you in her life."

Canyon shook his head. "I'm blessed to have her in mine."

Pruitt pushed back the brim of his regulation hat. "Were you aware there's a search and rescue civil aviation unit on the Shore? They assist law enforcement, the Guard and harbor police with certain situations. Always looking for a few good pilots—" he shot a look at Canyon "—and good men like you to join their ranks."

He thought of Hap Wallace and his own tumbleweed grandfather in the Civilian Air Patrol. "I didn't realize that was still an ongoing thing."

"I hope you'll consider it." Pruitt stuck out his hand. "Pleased to have you back in the Kiptohanock fold, neighbor."

Canyon stared at the deputy's hand for a second and then grasped it. "I'll be in touch." He swallowed. "Neighbor."

Pruitt returned to laying down the law with Randolph,

and Canyon headed down the hall to find Gray and his mother.

This day was turning out to be full of surprises.

In one of the curtained cubicles, Kristina sat beside Gray's empty hospital bed. Suffering from dehydration and hypothermia, he'd been taken upstairs to get an MRI to make sure there'd been no brain trauma.

She'd come too close to losing her son. Too close to losing all that remained of his father, Paxton Montgomery. Kristina felt she'd lived a thousand lifetimes of fear and sorrow since she drove Gray to the dance. Underneath her shirt, the dog tags lay heavy against her skin. Cold. Lifeless.

The weight of grief hung like an anchor around her neck. Pax would've been ashamed of how she'd hidden from the world since he died. He would've wanted so much more for her than the empty future to which she'd consigned herself.

Pax hadn't been a man given to fear. That had been her job in the marriage—to worry and wait for him to come home.

She sank onto the mattress. Only Pax wasn't ever coming home again. Not to her. He'd already gone home—to his truest home.

Her hand fisted around his dog tags. Now it was his turn to wait. For her.

And then the tears came. Tortured, racking sobs. The wrenching pain in her heart stole her breath.

She doubled over, wetting the pillowcase with her tears. For what was and for what could never be again.

At least, never again with Pax. He was gone. No matter how hard she tried to keep hold of him and what they'd been to each other, life—her life—marched on.

The finality of his leave-taking overcame her in a way she'd been unwilling to face before. She remembered the words Reverend Parks read at the Good Friday service, which seemed a lifetime ago.

Why do you seek the living among the dead?

Her heart constricted. Exactly what she'd been doing since Pax left her. She shook her head. Her hair loosened from the ponytail to fall across her face.

Pax hadn't left her and Gray. He'd died. But she and Gray weren't dead. Only an incredibly stupid person looked for life among those who were dead.

She pushed the hair out of her face. It was time—past time—she stopped. That she started living again. That she looked for life and love among the living.

It was time—a sob hiccuped out of her throat—time to say goodbye. Pax had lived and died with courage. And as his beloved widow, she could do no less than to live the rest of her days with courage, too.

She understood now with crystal clarity the truth of Margaret's wise advice. To miss Pax always, but to let him go.

Kristina squeezed her eyes shut. It hurt so much. "Oh, God, I don't want to let him go. I loved him so much." Her inadvertent cry echoed beyond the thin wall of fabric.

Flinching, she clapped her hand over her mouth. *Loved.* Past tense. Because life must always be lived in the present.

It was time to press forward. Onward and upward. To do anything else was to stagnate in a living death. A dishonor to Pax and what they'd been to each other.

Her hand shook as she lifted the chain off her neck. She couldn't bear this stranglehold of death any longer. She'd put the dog tags in a safe place for Gray to honor his father's memory.

But she must embrace life. A life she knew with certainty must involve Canyon. Her heart quickened at what he meant to her, the second chance for life and love he offered.

Two incredibly different men. One with a deceptively

invincible aura. The other with so many raw wounds. But both of whom loved her.

Had she been wrong? Was it possible to have two great loves in a lifetime? Her mouth trembled at the thought of a new life with Canyon. Like beholding a sunrise after a long, dark night. God had been so very good to her. The glorious hope of spring after the stark death of winter.

She held Pax's dog tags in her palm. With her finger, she traced his name imprinted on the metal. She had to do this now, before Gray returned. Before she lost her courage.

"Goodbye, my love," she whispered.

Closing her eyes, she blocked everything from her consciousness except for Pax. One last time. Just her and him.

The memory of his dark brown eyes. The laughing, playful flirtatiousness that had characterized their relationship from the first moment they met. The shining pride in his face the first time he held their son.

A curtain rustled.

She brushed her lips across the dog tags in her hand. "You are the love of my life, Paxton Montgomery. There will never be anyone like you."

There was nothing, she realized, like a first love. But thank God for His grace, Pax wouldn't remain her only love.

"I will never forget you." Her voice strengthened, taking on a fierceness. "I will always love you, Pax."

"—safe and sound to your mom. Oh, excuse me, Mrs. Montgomery."

Kristina's eyes snapped open. In the opened curtain stood Canyon. And behind him, the radiology technician with Gray in a wheelchair. Disoriented, she blinked at the look on Canyon's face...

Reality rushed back in a flood of sight and sound. The anguish in his eyes drove a dagger into her heart.

How long had he been standing there? What had he overheard? If he'd only just arrived, he might think—

"Canyon!"

She clambered off the bed. But he wheeled and blun-
dered past a startled Gray.

"What's wrong, Mom?" Gray pressed his hands flat on
the armrests and started to rise.

The tech put a firm hand on his shoulder. "Not so fast."

Kristina stepped outside the curtain. "I have to—"

"Mom, is everything okay? Why are your eyes so
puffy?"

She dodged Gray's outstretched hand. "I'll be right
back."

But she'd delayed too long. Canyon must've raced downstairs to the parking lot. From a window, she watched him
stride out of the hospital and get into his Jeep.

Too late again? In a tangle of emotions, she watched him
drive away. His vehicle disappeared out of sight as the sun
began its golden descent to the west.

Chapter Eighteen

When Canyon returned to the hospital with Jade's clothes, it was dark. And she was exhausted by the time they made the short trip home.

Home. For a brief, stupid day, he'd actually dared to believe he'd finally found his.

But after putting Jade to bed, he sat alone at the kitchen table. With two sleepless nights in a row, he was feeling raw and more than a little punchy.

He gazed out the window at the night sky to where the waning moon hung over the airfield. He hadn't meant to eavesdrop. But Kristina's words had left his heart frozen, rooted in place and unable to break free.

Ironic, considering he was the one who longed for wings.

He also arrived at several inescapable conclusions as he listened to the lonely sound of the wind sighing among the trees.

The hole Paxton Montgomery left in her heart was too big to be filled by him. He—who once longed to remain an emotional island—wanted nothing more than for his life to be filled with a couple of teenagers and the only woman he'd ever love.

His splendid isolation had been bridged. There'd be no going back. He was used to not being enough. What surprised him was how his inadequacy continued to hurt so much.

"God, what do I do now?" he whispered.

At 2:00 a.m., he remembered his buddy's text. And it seemed to Canyon that God—and the National Park Service—had thrown him a much-needed lifeline. A temporary reprieve, but a reprieve nonetheless.

Powering his phone, he quickly responded to his buddy's text and then shut down his phone again. If only he could shut off the pain of his love for Kristina as easily. If only he could reconcile himself to the rest of his life. A life without Kristina.

He wasn't sure how he could continue to live next door, seeing her on a daily basis. Being so close and yet so far from everything he wanted with her. He wanted a life with her.

About 5:00 a.m., Jade stumbled into the kitchen in her bathrobe and pajamas.

He staggered to his feet. "Does something hurt? Are you sick?"

"I'm fine." She frowned. "Why are you sitting in the dark?" She flicked the switch.

Grunting, he threw up his hand to protect his eyes.

Coming around the chair, she draped her arms around his neck. "What's going on?"

He told her about the text.

Sucking in a breath, she dropped her arms. "You're leaving me?"

He reached for her hand. "I'll only be gone a few weeks. The wildfires started early this season."

She backed away. "You said you and me...we'd stick together."

"We talked about me being gone the usual two weeks in July. This just moves up the timetable. I'll be back, I promise."

Her mouth hardened. "That's what Brandi always said."

"Two weeks, honey. That's all."

She gave him an elaborate, see-if-I-care shrug. "Right…"

"Look at me, honey." He tilted her chin till her gaze locked on to his. "You and me are for life."

She searched his face. "Really?"

"You're not getting rid of me that easily, kid." He somehow managed a smile. "Or at least not until you fly toward the beautiful life God's got in store for you, leaving your old man in the dust."

"Let me come with you."

Canyon sighed. "You can't miss school. Maybe you could stay with Margaret. She'd love the company."

"What about Kristina?"

He gave Jade a redacted version of what he overheard.

"I'm sure she didn't mean it the way it sounded. You must've misunderstood."

"Not much chance of misinterpreting what I heard."

Jade frowned. "You should tell her how you feel."

"I've said everything there is to say on my end. And she's made it perfectly clear there can never be a future between us."

Jade planted her hands on her hips. "You two are so perfect for each other."

"Two weeks is all I'm asking, sweetheart. Space to work things out in my head."

She scrunched her face. "What does that mean? What are you going to work out?"

"I wish I knew. That's why I need time."

He grabbed her in a bear hug. She made a halfhearted attempt to pull away. "I'm still your dad, right?"

"A bossy one." She blew out a dramatic breath. "But I guess we're stuck with each other now, huh?"

"You got that right."

She looked at him out of those big green eyes of hers. "This has something to do with the Easter photo of Grandma Eileen you left on my dresser."

He moved toward the window. "It's time to break the Collier curse for good, Jade. I can't become Kristina's Hap Wallace. I won't allow what happened to my mother to ruin your life, too."

"I'd still like us to attend the sunrise service together before you go. One of the better Collier traditions. Please?"

He was bound to see Kristina and Gray there. No chance of avoiding them. But Jade asked so little of him. He wouldn't—couldn't—deny her this.

"I won't change my mind about leaving, Jade."

She cinched the belt of her bathrobe around her waist. "I know. But I like the idea of us greeting Resurrection Day together. A new start after last night. A new dawn. A new life."

Canyon wished he shared her optimism. He felt old. Used up and worthless. Despite his efforts, helpless to change his destiny as a Collier. Did history always have to repeat itself?

He didn't bother to shave, but he put on a clean shirt and jeans. Jade surprised him. Her hair wound in a low bun, she donned a hunter-green corduroy dress over brown leggings. The color of the dress made her eyes appear as luminous as a tidal pool.

Some things hadn't changed, though. Like the black lipstick and fingernail polish. And the splash of magenta gleaming in her hair.

Vestiges of the real Jade. For which he was thankful. Her essence, uniquely and wondrously crafted by God.

She wobbled in her tall brown boots. "Do I look okay?" She grimaced. "Or dumb?"

"Better than okay." He threw out his arms. "Fabulous. Marvelous. Gorgeous."

"You're such a dad." She rolled her eyes. "No need to oversell it."

Canyon bit back a laugh and handed Jade her coat. "Even in April, it'll be cool with the wind blowing off the water."

He grabbed his favorite coat—Hap's well-worn, broken-in, super-comfortable leather flight jacket.

It'd be easy to settle into Hap's destiny. To love Kristina from afar. Stay here among new friends and church family.

He was so thankful to God for helping him find the kids before it was too late. God had already done the biggest search and rescue on his heart.

It was a short drive to the church parking lot. They shuffled toward the waterfront. Despite Margaret's beckoning, he settled on the perimeter of the seawall to view the sunrise. Always the outsider looking in.

The inexorable ebb and flow of the waves washed the beach below. Water slapped against the hulls of boats tied to slips in the marina. The American and Coast Guard flags snapped taut in the brisk sea breeze.

Only twenty-four hours had passed since he and Kristina watched the sunrise while they waited for news of their lost children. But a vast gulf now yawned between what was and what could never be.

Across the harbor and the shadowy outline of barrier islands, the horizon at the edge of the world began to lighten. No clouds in the darkened sky. The sunrise would be a beauty.

Cloistered with their family near the adjacent Coastie pier, Sawyer and Seth waved. For the first time, he felt a kinship with Kiptohanock watermen like Seth Duer. Men who earned their living based on their understanding of the elements of sea and sky.

His internal radar went on full alert as he spotted Kristina standing between her brother, Weston, and Gray. Reverend Parks strode toward the mounted bell used in times of maritime disaster at the end of the pier.

Canyon's breath sent puffs of air into the April morning. In the coolness of the predawn hour, he appreciated the warmth of Hap's jacket. Like the airfield, part of his legacy.

Jade would always be his most important Collier legacy. She tucked her arm into the crook in his elbow. And when he contemplated how close he'd come to losing her, his stomach knotted.

Blinking past those inconveniently timed allergies, he draped his arm across her shoulders.

She patted his coat. "I wish you'd talk to Kristina."

His lips, stiff and cold, brushed against the top of her hair. "Kristina doesn't want me."

"She's staring at you." Jade poked him in the side. "Look. I think she wants to talk."

Instead, he fixed his gaze on the church steeple. "Only thing I ever had to offer her was a messed-up family heritage. It's for the best. I could never compare to Gray's father."

"You don't have to be anybody but yourself." She jabbed him with her bony elbow this time. "Canyon Collier is more than good enough, in my completely unbiased opinion."

Her confidence warmed a few of the places in his heart that had grown numb over the years.

Canyon smiled. "You are totally biased, but I love you, Jade Collier, for your faith in me."

"Kristina's in love with you." Jade's gaze bored into him. "I wish you'd allow yourself the possibility of what you two could be together."

He wished they'd stop talking about this. "It's not that easy."

She tapped her boot on the pavement. "Why does your relationship with Kristina have to be so hard?"

"And what makes you the expert on relationships?"

She smirked. "I had a front-row seat with Beech and Brandi on how not to do relationships."

Canyon reckoned she had at that.

Her lips twisted. "Poor Hap Wallace and Grandma Eileen. The Collier family track record with love leaves a lot to be desired."

Maybe it would be better to get away from here. Start fresh somewhere else. Better for Jade? Or for him? Was he being selfish?

"Be the first to break the cycle, Jade."

She leaned against him. "I've decided Gray's not as geeky as I first believed. When he didn't ask me to the dance, I might've been too hasty in writing him off."

"Ya think?"

"He's smart and sweet and kind."

Canyon raised his eyebrows. "What's not to love, right?"

She glanced at him sideways, letting him know she was aware of being gently mocked. "Gray's got a lot of potential. We make a good team. Besides, next growth spurt he's bound to fill out and be less skinny. What do you think?"

"I think..." He'd rather not contemplate Jade in a more grown-up relationship, even if the guy was Grayson Montgomery. "I think one day Gray may surprise you."

He gave Jade a swift kiss on her forehead.

"What's that for?"

"For being you."

"Whatever. Oh, hey. Look." She nudged him.

A fiery rim of orange topped the watery expanse. There were indrawn breaths. His included. A profound silence hung as if all of creation held its breath, too. As it had, perhaps, on the first resurrection morning.

Waiting. Yearning. Straining for the light of day. For hope to be fulfilled. For death to be vanquished. For life to triumph.

The air pulsed with color. And then the wait was over. Light burst forth into a glorious dayspring.

Pink streaked the indigo sky. A molten path of red stretched from the foaming surf on the beach to the heart of the golden orb rising from the darkness of night. And he became aware that for resurrection day to truly come, the darkness of Good Friday first had to precede it.

Something trilled in his soul. Something he'd longed for his whole life. Something more than himself. For Someone more than himself.

At last, his restlessness satisfied. Quenched not with earthly passion. Or family. Or purpose.

In that second, he knew neither Kristina nor Gray nor Jade was the answer to his heart's stirrings. Only this One who'd conquered sin and death forever. Who—if there'd been no other as wicked as Canyon—would've died, gone to the grave and risen for him alone.

Reverend Parks started a hymn. Among the faithful, their voices swelled, a rising tide of acclamation.

Seth Duer and his gravelly smoker's voice. Margaret Davenport's determined alto. Evy Pruitt's sweet soprano. His stumbling contribution.

Blending. Mixing. Until he could no longer distinguish one voice from the other.

He thought of his dear grandmother on a long-ago, wartime Easter, standing between the two men who would love her most.

A crescendo of praise winged across the harbor. Echoing across the ages. Culminating with him and Jade today. An unbroken anthem.

He had no idea what tomorrow would bring. No idea what would become of them. But though he might never be enough for Kristina, Canyon was possessed of a sudden certainty that God was.

And within Canyon, God would be enough for everything—past, present and future.

Reverend Parks's voice rang out. "He is risen."

Canyon lifted his head. For the first time in his misbegotten life, Canyon actually believed it. "He is risen indeed."

After a brief seaside prayer, Reverend Parks directed the congregation to the fellowship hall for coffee and Long Johns.

Kristina hung back as Gray and her brother's family headed for the church. Weaving around 'come heres and 'been heres, she resolved to allow nothing else to stand between her and the man she most wanted to see.

She'd gotten trapped at the hospital pending Gray's MRI results. She'd tried calling Canyon but got his voice mail every time. Once the hospital released Gray around midnight, her son had insisted they drive over to the airfield.

But the Collier residence was dark. And she was too overwrought from the events of the past twenty-four hours to do anything but go home.

Probably for the best. Better to set things straight with Canyon after a good night's sleep when they could both think clearly. Yet she'd lain awake, coming to grips with what she needed to say to him.

Losing sight of him for a second, she finally located the Colliers on the periphery of the thinning crowd. If she had her way, she'd make it her life's mission to ensure Canyon and Jade were never relegated to the outskirts of the crowd—or life—ever again.

She'd hurt Canyon without meaning to. He wasn't the strong, immovable rock he liked people to believe. She knew this because—of all the people in the world—he'd opened himself to her.

Knowledge was power, a power he'd willingly given her. She likewise had the power to wound him the most. It wasn't a power she took lightly.

She'd replayed over and over what she'd said at the hospital and how it must've sounded to him. She needed to explain not only the words, but the thoughts behind her words.

Kristina hoped he'd give them a second chance.

As she approached, Jade let go of her uncle. "I'll leave you guys to talk." She picked her way toward the fellowship hall.

Kristina took a breath. "Canyon, we need to talk about what you thought you heard at the hospital yesterday." She reached for him.

He moved out of her reach. "I know what I heard. And I'll deal with it."

This was not going in the direction she'd hoped. "I didn't mean to hurt you."

"Don't worry about it." He grimaced. "I'm tough. As a Collier, I've had to be. Some things don't change."

She stiffened. "If you'd stop feeling sorry for yourself and listen—"

"You'd be the expert on pity parties, wouldn't you?"

She gasped.

This was getting out of hand. She forced herself to take a few slow, calming breaths. He was only reacting out of hurt and wrong information.

"What happened to talking to the real estate agent?" He jabbed his thumb toward the empty storefront. "What happened to moving on?"

She understood what he was doing. This was about deflecting his hurt. "Are we talking about florist shops or something else?"

"What happened to making a new life for yourself?"

She crossed her arms. "You promised you wouldn't push."

Canyon shook his head. "The only one who doesn't believe you're ready is you. And until you decide to move forward, there's nothing anyone can say or do that will make the least difference in the world."

Her eyes widened. "Why has this suddenly become 'love me, love my florist shop'?"

Canyon ran his hand through his hair. "Fact is, you'll never be ready. That's the real truth, isn't it, Kristina?"

She raised her chin. "We're both tired. We shouldn't be having this conversation now." Her eyes darted left and right. "Much less in the middle of the town."

"The time and place are never going to be right for us." He squeezed his eyes shut and opened them. "And I'm not willing to settle for second best this time. Not with you."

"If you'd just let me explain what I was thinking and feeling—"

He folded his arms across his chest. "Start with how you feel about me, Kristina."

And there it was—the moment of truth. The moment to say out loud what she'd only begun to acknowledge in the secret places of her heart. She stood on the precipice of something new.

But the old Kristina warred with the Kristina she longed to be. Hesitating. Afraid to commit herself. Scared to step off the ledge. Terrified she'd fall.

"We have two children's lives to consider," she whispered.

"Do you love me, Kristina?"

She opened her mouth and closed it again. "I think we should go slow."

"We go any slower and we'll be moving in reverse." He scrubbed his hand over his face. "You still can't say the words to me, can you?"

She squared her jaw. "You said you'd wait for me. That you'd allow me to take as much time as I needed." She quivered. "I took off the dog tags, Canyon. I'm trying."

"Congratulations." His mouth contorted. "I'm thick, but I've finally learned my lesson. You, Kristina Montgomery, choose roots, never wings. You prefer winter to spring. And you always will."

"Don't be this way, Canyon." She grabbed for his arm. "If you'd only be patient a little while longer—"

He wrenched away. "I'm heading out of state to fight wildfires for a few weeks." His mouth drooped. "Time for clarity. Time to surrender foolish dreams that'll never have any basis in reality."

"You're leaving?" She stared at him. "What about Jade? What about us? Wildfires aren't safe."

"According to you, there is no us." His eyes flashed. "You're the one who's not safe. There's no safe landing zone with you."

His words cut like a sharp blade. "Aerial application isn't the only thing you're an expert at, Canyon." Her nostrils flared. "Avoidance, too."

Canyon shrugged. "Like you, old habits die hard. I'll return to fulfill the rest of my contracts with area farmers. After I've had time to sort through what I want for my future and Jade's."

Tears burned the back of her eyelids. "You promised you wouldn't give up on us. You promised."

He looked at her then, long and hard, with those sky-blue eyes that tore at her heart. Anger and hurt. Hurt beyond repair?

"I said I'd never give up on us as long as I was sure you'd be waiting for me at the end of the day."

Her heart thudded.

The anger drained from his face. Only the sadness remained. His shoulders slumped.

"And of that I'm can no longer be sure." He took a step. "I have arrangements to make with Margaret."

Clutching her arms around her body, she couldn't hold back the tears. "Canyon…"

"Goodbye, Kris."

This time, he walked away from her.

Chapter Nineteen

On the ridge below, the silver foil shelters glinted amid the raging inferno. Sizing up the situation, Canyon decided he couldn't land the Bell helo he'd borrowed from the Forest Service when the distress call came in to base camp.

The wildfire had jumped the break the hotshots had created. Within sight of base camp, an unexpected flare-up had cut off the half dozen men. They'd raced uphill only to become trapped by the dense forest erupting into flames. Out of options, they deployed their shelters. Hunkered down, they prepared for the worst.

From his vantage point in the sky, he could see the flames hurtling through the trees. Coming too hot and too fast. The firefighters wouldn't survive.

The trees caught fire, popping like firecrackers. He had to get out of here. He couldn't hold this position. The howling wind—whipped into a fury by the blazing heat—buffeted the chopper.

And in that split second, he had a choice.

His heart ratcheted. His thoughts flew to Jade. To Kristina and Gray. What about them?

Yet the brave men on the ground had children and sweethearts, too. He couldn't get another picture out of his mind—the Easter sunrise over the harbor. And the One who'd also made a painful choice to give Canyon new life.

His hand steadied on the stick. His heart settled into

a regular rhythm. There was one chance. An open area, which he believed would slow the fire long enough for the crew to reach another clearing.

A safe zone in which he could land. If the crew could make it there in time. The urgency mounted.

He made a risky, life-altering decision. If he was wrong…they'd all die. He swallowed past the bile clogging his throat.

Reaching, he keyed the radio. Hovering low, he called to the fire crew on the ground. "Get out of the shelters. Follow me and run."

The crew threw off their shelters. Blades whirring, he led the way toward the lone uninvolved path to safety. As the crew cleared the conflagration, a tree to his right exploded like a matchstick, shattering the air in a sonic boom. The chopper whiplashed.

Gritting his teeth, he fought to control the bucking helo. He was too low. The fire was too close. He was going down…

On day seventeen of Canyon's trip, Kristina found herself on the flagstone terrace of Inglenook having tea. She frowned into her cup. She'd begun to think of Canyon's absence as an exile.

He was already three days past his deadline for returning home. For returning to Jade, as he'd promised. But not to her. He'd made that much perfectly clear.

There was no her and him. No them. From his nightly phone calls to Jade—Gray kept Kristina informed—Canyon blamed his continuing absence on the sudden outbreak of a new fire.

Everyone in Kiptohanock followed news accounts of the raging inferno. The networks replayed the footage of men trapped on a mountain with no hope of escape. Until the blue-and-white helicopter guided them to a safe landing zone.

The rescue made national headlines. She believed her heart might stop the first time she viewed the clip. Because it also revealed what a close call it had been for Canyon, too.

"A singular act of courage," one network anchor called Canyon's heroism.

"Going beyond the call of duty to help those who couldn't help themselves," the captain of the rescued fire crew declared.

Earning media-shy Canyon Collier a commendation from the US Forest Service, a Pilot of the Year award from the international aviation association and an invitation to the White House.

Kristina alternated between being proud and worried for his safety. In other words, she spent a lot of time on her knees.

She missed Jade, living for the duration at Inglenook. Which sounded as if Jade were incarcerated with Margaret. Not the case at all. To hear Gray tell it, Jade and Margaret were having a blast.

Most of all, she missed Canyon. Kristina set the cup into the saucer with a clatter.

"That cup belonged to my great-grandmother." Margaret rested against the cushion in the scrolled iron chair. "I'd like to think it will survive another generation, if you please."

Kristina was about done being a doormat. "Why did you invite me here?"

"Testy these days, aren't you, dear? Feeling lovelorn?"

Kristina pushed against the table. The chair scraped across the flagstone. "I think we're finished."

Margaret laid her hand over Kristina's.

Half in, half out of her chair, she froze at the usually aloof woman's surprising touch.

"I'm sorry." Margaret patted her hand. "Forgive me for

the habits of a lifetime. I'm trying to change." She gave Kristina a rueful smile. "Having Jade here these last few weeks has been such a joy. And set so many things right in my own mind."

An apology? From Margaret Davenport? Stunned, Kristina sank into the chair.

She gripped the iron armrests, the metallic surface cold against her palms. "Is this about Canyon?"

Margaret's elegantly clad shoulders rose and fell. "Not entirely. But I'll eventually get around to him, of course."

Which made about as much sense as Kristina's contrary refusal to admit her love for Canyon on Easter morning.

She'd had seventeen long days to berate herself for relapsing into stupid fears. "What's this about, Margaret?"

"After my mother passed, I was all Canyon's grandmother had left. Hap had died. Canyon was stationed off-Shore with the Guard. You know about Beech."

Kristina folded her hands in her lap.

Margaret's gaze drifted to the cordgrass waving in the marshy inlet. "Eileen was alone so much with only her flowers for comfort." Her mouth tightened.

Kristina figured Margaret knew something about being lonely. She wondered how much time Margaret had spent alone in this magnificent tidewater mansion. Regretting missed opportunities. Like Kristina regretted hers.

"Eileen never got over believing Freddie Collier would wing his way home one day."

Kristina thought of the hours she'd spent gazing at the sky over the last few days. Anxious for the sound of Canyon's plane. Wondering when he'd return.

Margaret's face grew pensive. "A delusion made worse, I always believed, because of the lack of a body for closure."

"You and Canyon's mother must've been about the same age."

"In the youth group." She gave Kristina a wry smile. "If you can imagine old fogies like us being teenagers."

Margaret dropped her gaze. "Amber couldn't wait to leave Kiptohanock. To escape her mother's overwhelming grief. She inherited a wanderlust from her father. His absence shadowed both their lives. It doesn't take a psychologist to understand Amber's self-destructive choices."

Kristina's stomach churned as she remembered one of Canyon's painful admissions. Neither he nor his brother ever knew their father.

Margaret shook her head. "The kind of love Eileen felt for Freddie Collier...so all-consuming." Her eyes locked on Kristina's. "Not meant to be given to any mortal. A love that should only be given to God."

Kristina bit her lip.

Margaret exhaled. "Beech acted out to get attention. Good or bad, he didn't care. As long as he got someone's attention. As for Canyon, thank God for Hap. He was the making of the boy."

Yes, thank God for Hap Wallace. Because Canyon Collier was indeed a wonderful man. The best. Something she'd known to be true before he ever rescued those men.

Her hero. And Gray's. Most definitely Jade's. If only Canyon could see himself as they saw him.

"I know what it's like to lose someone you love, Kristina."

She remembered the odd conversation with Seth Duer at the pancake supper. That everyone had their own battles to fight and wars to overcome.

"One of the things I've learned the hard way is a verse that talks about leaving the past and pressing forward to what lies ahead."

"Good advice," Kristina whispered. "If only I knew how. I messed up everything with Canyon."

"How badly do you want to move forward, Kristina?"

She glanced over the patio. "I don't think he'll forgive me."

"I believe in second chances. I think Canyon does, too." Margaret squeezed Kristina's hand. "And when you're blessed with someone to move forward with, you must run toward him.

Kristina tilted her head. "To run and not grow faint... to soar like an eagle."

Margaret let go of her hand. "I'm the one who found Eileen."

Kristina's heart thudded. "The day she died?"

"I'd begged her to live with me, but Eileen always told me..." Margaret's voice wobbled. "She told me she had to be there to welcome Freddie when he returned home."

After what Pax's sweet father had suffered with the dementia, Kristina hated that terrible, terrible disease.

"I went over to the bungalow every day." A tear trailed down Margaret's cheek. "She'd go silent in the middle of a conversation, tilt her ear toward the ceiling or rush out into the yard at the sound of an airplane. Listening for him."

Kristina swallowed. And recalled Canyon's remark about his grandmother's white garden planted as a marker.

"Of course, it was never him. She'd snap out of it after a moment and smile. 'Next time. He's close. I can feel it.'"

Suppose Kristina never heard the sound of Canyon's plane again? Suppose he never came back? Her temples pounded. But he must. If not for her, then certainly for Jade.

"I awoke early one morning to the strangest feeling." Margaret fretted the cuff of her silk blouse. "I couldn't get Eileen off my mind. I rushed over to her house in my housecoat and slippers."

Kristina pictured the usually immaculate, always in-control Margaret disheveled and scared.

"I panicked and called for her. But the house was deserted. The door wide open. That's when I knew."

Kristina tensed. "Knew what?"

"I knew where to find her." Margaret stared across the tidal creek. "I'd found her there before, after a restless night. I ran through the woods toward the airfield. It had been abandoned since Hap's death. Potholes in the asphalt, weeds growing through the cracks…"

How hard Canyon must've worked to bring the airfield to its current pristine condition. No wonder he was proud of his business.

"…and there at the end of the runway, she rested against the old sycamore tree—" Margaret's voice cracked.

Kristina's heart broke at Margaret's remembered pain and of the old woman so alone.

Margaret gulped. "I have no idea where Eileen got them. She must've spent the entire night planting them."

Kristina had missed something. "Planting what?"

"Eileen had lined both sides of the runway with tiny American flags. When I arrived, the flags fluttered in the wind."

Kristina leaned forward. "But what about Eileen?"

Margaret's eyes shone. "Her face was upturned to the golden glow of the sun, serene at last. Her eyes were closed. Her body still warm to the touch."

"Her soul flown to heaven's beckoning call," Kristina whispered.

And very deliberately, she forever replaced the hideous image she'd carried—burning, jagged metal raining over a windswept Afghan mountain—with a new one of Pax.

Margaret took a ragged breath. "Did she hear Freddie's plane? Is that why she went out there? To welcome him home?"

Kristina reached across the table and clasped Margaret's hand.

"Fanciful, but I know in my heart she and her great love are together again at last."

Tears slid down Kristina's cheeks.

"I pray, Kristina, you will not allow happiness to slide from your grasp—"

"He left me, remember?"

Margaret's mouth thinned. "Are you talking about your dead husband or are you referring to Canyon?"

"I'll always love Pax, but I've let him go. I'm ready to move forward into a new life with Canyon."

"Does he know how you feel?"

"Things escalated so fast." Kristina blinked. "And then he was gone."

"I told you about Eileen because I wanted you to understand the baggage he carries. The insecurity he feels. Given the example of his grandmother and Hap, he believes his love for you could never compare to the love you and your husband once shared."

"That's not true." She clutched the edge of the table. "Pax is my past. But Canyon is my future. I know that now. I love him. But we got into this stupid argument..." Her throat closed.

"If that's how you feel, then you must come up with a way to help him see the truth, Kristina."

From inside, the doorbell chimed just as Kristina's cell beeped. Rising, Margaret disappeared into the house. Kristina rummaged through the purse stashed beside the chair.

"Hello? Jade— Where—"

She frowned, trying to make sense of the girl's garbled, rapid-fire speech. "What? Is something—"

Margaret and Honey strolled onto the patio.

Kristina's gut tightened as comprehension dawned. "Canyon called to tell you he's coming home?" Her heart fluttered like the wings of a hummingbird. "This afternoon?"

Promising to call again later, she clicked Off. Her hand trembled.

Margaret's penciled eyebrows arched. "What do you want to do, Kristina?"

"I want a life with Canyon." She pushed back her shoulders. "I want to give him the happily-ever-after we both deserve."

Margaret smiled. "How can I help?"

A sudden crazy notion took hold of Kristina. A sure-fire way to get his attention. Perhaps the only thing that might stand a chance of convincing Canyon how much she loved him. How much she'd staked on a future with him. To help him see himself through not only her eyes but the town's also.

"I need to cut some flowers in my garden." She stood. "A lot of flowers. I'll also need yards of ribbon."

Margaret steepled her bejeweled hands under her chin. "I think I see where you're going with this. A hero's welcome. Consider my garden at your disposal."

Kristina shook her head. "But it's Garden Week. The judges will be here tomorrow."

Margaret shrugged. "There's always next year."

A crease puckered Honey's forehead. "If y'all are talking about what I think you're talking about, count the flowers from the inn's garden, too."

Margaret sniffed. "Without Inglenook, the trophy will be yours."

Honey batted her lashes. "I prefer to win my laurels fair and square, thank you all the same. Like you said, there's always next year. Right now, we need to be good neighbors."

Margaret raised her fist as if rallying the troops. "Kiptohanock must welcome home our hero."

"Exactly." Honey whipped her phone out of her pocket. "I'll text my sisters. Evy, too."

"I'll telephone Agnes Parks, the rest of the guild and my book club." Margaret hurried to a table inside the patio doors. "We need to buy every flower at the other two florist shops on the peninsula, pronto." She poked her head out the door. "Call your dad, Honey. He'll know what to do. Between him and the other watermen, they'll set the village to rights."

"On it." Honey tapped her foot as she dialed another number. "I'll call the florists and tell them to reserve…"

Kristina's head whirled. Each woman a separate force of nature. And having marshaled forces, unstoppable.

"But I can't afford—"

"On my credit card, of course." Margaret waved her hand.

"I can't let you—"

"Kristina!" Margaret bellowed.

She and Honey jolted.

"Do you love this young man or not?"

To someone of Margaret's age, she and Canyon must appear so young. As for so in love?

Oh, how she hoped so.

Chapter Twenty

In the translucent glow of the late-afternoon sun, the barrier islands gleamed like strung pearls along the Delmarva Peninsula.

Following the coastline, Canyon brought the plane low as if skimming the frothing waves. Shorebirds dotted the sandy beaches.

He imagined his grandfather sighting the pristine shoreline after a hazardous journey chasing German subs. The joy, the anticipation, the rightness of coming home at last.

Yet unlike his grandfather, no special love waited for him. Never would. In the ways that mattered, Canyon was nothing like his grandfather.

Sure, he loved the thrill and freedom of flying through the skies. But if Kristina had offered him the kind of love his grandmother gave Freddie Collier, nothing could've induced Canyon to leave Kiptohanock or Kristina ever again.

To his right, the blue-green hue of the ocean glimmered. To his left lay the tree-studded inland horizon. Despite the loneliness facing him, his heart felt a ridiculous surge of gladness.

For the first time, he realized he'd come full circle. Found a home where he'd first begun. And even without Kristina, he was determined to make a better life for Jade.

In everything but blood, she was already his daughter. On the mountain, he'd vowed—if he could take off once more and safely land at base camp with the men—to make it a reality on paper, too.

His heart hurt thinking of Kristina and Gray. Thinking of the relationship he'd never experience with either of them. He would've loved becoming a father figure to the teenage boy.

As for Kristina? Some dreams were never meant to be fulfilled.

He'd left the Shore to wrap his mind around how he could continue to live next door to the only woman he'd ever love, knowing she'd never love him.

But he was coming home—in the truest sense of the word—even without Kristina in his life. Home, where he belonged. He brought the plane to a higher altitude as he approached the outline of the Kiptohanock harbor.

Canyon had thought about a lot of things over the last few weeks. He'd considered selling everything and relocating himself and Jade somewhere else. Anywhere else.

He hadn't welcomed the publicity over the rescue, but now he'd have his choice of plum opportunities. Aerial application specialists were suddenly a hot commodity.

And a new dream had arisen. A dream of training a whole new generation of ag pilots. He'd cautiously investigated a flight instructor position with an old friend who ran a training academy in Georgia.

But in the end, Canyon didn't want to subject Jade to another upheaval. She'd tentatively found a place for herself in Kiptohanock. And he'd begun to suspect—despite her vehement denials—Jade was more attached to Gray Montgomery than she was yet willing to admit.

He also didn't want to yank her away from Kristina, the only positive female figure she'd ever had in her life. Nor from Margaret's grandmotherly influence.

Because of the children's friendship, he was bound to encounter Kristina far more than his comfort level or his heart wanted. But he'd resolved to put Jade's well-being first, not his own.

He'd never been responsible for another human being. At least not since he left the Shore and Beech went to jail.

Every night when he talked to Jade, they'd steered away from discussing Kristina, although this morning when he'd called to let her know his ETA, Jade had revealed Kristina had bought the storefront with plans to open a florist shop.

Canyon was happy for her. Glad she'd chosen to move on with her life. To pursue her dream. Even if that dream didn't include a life with him.

He had more to his life than the airfield, too. After the pancake supper, he'd been recruited by the volunteer fire department. And thanks to Pruitt, he'd enrolled in the SAR Civilian Aviation unit.

The church steeple appeared in his sights. Streaks of purple and indigo studded the sky. And something colorful fluttered from the town gazebo.

What in the world?

He pressed his face to the window, not believing his own eyes. Circling for another look, he buzzed the inlet.

The plane's shadow fell across the square. At the sound of the engine, people poured out of the café, the church and the library. The fire station, too.

Why were they waving small American flags? What was going on? It looked like a hero's welcome.

As for the gazebo?

Hundreds of red, white and blue ribbons were tied around every railing, every conceivable surface. He did a 180 to make another pass. Who was this for?

It couldn't be for him. He shook his head. Could it? Welcoming him home. It shouldn't be. But it was.

Canyon didn't feel like a hero. He'd only done what anyone else would've done, getting his buddies out of harm's way.

Seeing the townspeople—his people—welcoming an outsider like him home to Kiptohanock… He swallowed. Maybe only an outsider in his mind?

After one more loop around the green, he dipped the wing of the AT in grateful acknowledgment. Pulling up, he headed north. With a full heart, he left the fishing village behind for now.

Farther along the shoreline, he passed the Neck, where the lighthouse stood as it had for a hundred years, tall and proud. A beacon of hope. He sighed.

Canyon was determined to be the best dad Jade could have. He never wanted her to lack for anything again. His days of choosing avoidance were over.

It'd be dark soon. He needed to get home. To Jade. To the rest of his life.

Passing over the woods, he made adjustments to the controls as he neared the airstrip. But as he began the descent, his eyes widened. Hundreds more red, white and blue ribbons were tied around the trunk of the giant sycamore at the far end of the runway.

And white blooms edged both sides of the runway. Spelling out the words *Safe Landing*. His heart quickened. Who—

He lowered the landing gear. The wheels touched down and settled gently into the grip of gravity. He spotted a lone figure outside the hangar.

A beautiful blonde woman in a blue wraparound dress. Kristina. Waving at him. His vision swam.

He applied the brakes. The plane slowed. What was she doing here?

What was happening? Was he dreaming? If he was, then *please, God*, don't ever let him awake.

He cut the engine. The propellers continued to spin for a moment. Canyon's heart leaped in his chest.

Canyon eased open the door. Climbing onto the wing,

he jumped to the ground. She hadn't moved from where she waited. Did she wait for him?

She wrung her hands. Her china-blue eyes appeared large in her face. Tremulous with uncertainty.

A distance remained between them. An interminable length of space. A gulf he didn't know how to bridge.

But then she bridged it for him.

Why didn't he say something?

Kristina ached to embrace him, but he remained frozen beside the wing of the plane. Was he still so very angry with her? He looked more tired than the last time she saw him. Yet his eyes were as startling a blue as ever, a blue in which she'd willingly drown.

She'd been afraid he wouldn't arrive before the sun set to see the message. Did he not understand what was in her heart?

Her heart was full of him. When he walked away after the sunrise service, she'd been angry, confused and hurt. Why was he just standing there?

Perhaps her instincts were wrong. Perhaps he'd never loved her. Or at least didn't love her now.

Was Margaret right about his reluctance to share his feelings with her? Because of a false sense of unworthiness. How could she make him understand that the shadow of Pax would never again lie between them?

Canyon was her future. Hers and Gray's. Life belonged to the living. Her life and her love belonged to him. His for the taking.

Why didn't he move? Did he not understand what she'd spelled out on the ground? Why didn't he—

Kristina squared her shoulders. She was done with waiting for life to happen. She was done with life passing her by.

She was taking her life in her own capable hands. No

more waiting for the prince to mount a rescue. She was coming to his.

One step forward. Two. And then she was running.

Toward Canyon. Toward life. Toward love. Toward her future. A future she wanted more than anything else in the world.

With Canyon Collier, the Kiptohanock black sheep whose smile and laughter made her ache inside.

As if awaking from slumber, he took a disjointed step forward. Then another. His stride became longer and faster with each step. Crossing the distance between them, he swept her into his arms.

Laughing, crying, she wrapped her arms around his neck. "I love you. I love *you*, Canyon Collier. I love you so much."

He buried his face into her hair. "Kris. Oh, Kris."

"Jade told me she felt that you were always meant to be her dad. And she your daughter. That it was only a matter of time before God brought you together and you found each other."

Kristina drew her head back so she could look into his eyes. "There's no one for me but you." She held his face between her hands. "There's only you from now on." She bit her lip. "If you want me."

"I want you." His gaze locked on to hers. "I suspect I've loved you since the moment you nearly wrecked my plane."

She trembled at his touch. "I think I was always meant to love you. It was only a matter of time before God brought us together and we found each other."

His arms tightened around her. "I love you, Kris." His voice went ragged. "So much. Forever."

"I'm yours. Forever." She traced his jawline with her finger. "Me. Gray. The house. Everything."

When he looked at her, full of tenderness and passion,

she beheld a future full of beginnings. Blue skies, bright with promise.

"You. Me. Jade and Gray." His voice went husky, sending pleasurable swirls goose bumping along her arms. "Our house. Our airfield. Our florist shop."

Her eyes filled with tears. "You heard about me buying the shop?"

Canyon gave her that slow, lopsided smile. Her insides quivered. "Do you even know me, Kristina Montgomery?" His breath fanned her cheek. "I have teenage spies everywhere."

Smiling, she rose on her tiptoes and kissed him. "Kristina Collier, if you please."

"As marriage proposals go—" his hand swept the runway "—this one is tops. And yes, I accept."

She could feel the drumming of his heart through the fabric of his shirt. "God has been so good to me." She gave him a shaky laugh. "Two great loves in one lifetime."

His eyes went opaque. "You've made me the happiest man on earth."

She luxuriated in the feel of his arms around her. "Not as happy as me."

He leaned closer. "Where, dare I ask, are the children?"

She snuggled closer in his embrace. "At the house, waiting to celebrate our engagement. Their fingers are sore from tying all the ribbons."

He cupped her cheek. "Sure of yourself, weren't you?"

She brushed her mouth against his palm. "The only thing I'm sure of is I never want to spend another day without you."

The look on his face almost broke her heart. As if he'd never believed she would love him. As if he'd believed no one would ever love him.

"You'd be okay spending your life waiting for another pilot to come home?"

"Canyon Collier, you are so worth waiting for. Besides, there are far worse things in life than always having to look up."

"I'm going to spend the rest of my life loving you, Kris."

"Welcome home, my darling." She pushed a strand of hair off his forehead. "Welcome home."

* * * * *

If you loved this tale of sweet romance,
pick up these other stories
from author Lisa Carter

COAST GUARD COURTSHIP
COAST GUARD SWEETHEART
FALLING FOR THE SINGLE DAD
THE DEPUTY'S PERFECT MATCH

Available now from Love Inspired!

Find more great reads at www.LoveInspired.com

Dear Reader,

I don't know about you, but I've always had a hard time letting go. Letting go of the past. Letting go of those I've loved. Letting go of dreams.

It's not hard for me to let go of the bad. My challenge often comes in letting go of that which has been good, fruitful and purpose driven in my life. I tend to cling to the past good, unable and unwilling to move forward because of a fear that the new will not prove as wonderful and satisfying as the old.

This book was written during a season of change for me. A time of transition after the death of my father, for whom I'd spent the majority of the last two years caring. A season of approaching empty nest, with one child already in college and the youngest in her senior year of high school. A change in ministry focus. In other words, a lot of change in almost every aspect of my life.

I hate change. But as Kristina discovers, it is impossible to remain in the past. To refuse to move forward is to stagnate and die—mentally, spiritually and emotionally. When we refuse to fully cross over the threshold of God's open door, we are in effect saying we don't trust Him to have our best interests at heart. And what I've learned in this season of great change in my life is that God always keeps His children close to His heart.

I hope you have enjoyed taking this journey with me, Canyon and Kristina. I would love to hear from you. You may email me at lisa@lisacarterauthor.com or visit www.lisacarterauthor.com.

Wishing you fair winds and following seas,
Lisa Carter

AMISH CHRISTMAS TWINS
Christmas Twins • by Patricia Davids

After returning to her Amish community, pregnant widow and mom of twins Willa Chase is devastated when her grandfather turns her away. An accident strands her at the home of John Miller—jolting the reclusive widower out of sorrow and into a Christmas full of joy and hope for a second chance at family.

THE RANCHER'S MISTLETOE BRIDE
Wyoming Cowboys • by Jill Kemerer

Managing Lexi Harrington's newly inherited ranch through the holidays might not have been cowboy Clint Romine's brightest idea. Getting close to her means revealing secrets he's long kept hidden. And falling for her means he'll have to convince Lexi her home isn't back in the big city—but in his arms.

AN ALASKAN CHRISTMAS
Alaskan Grooms • by Belle Calhoune

Single mom Maggie Richards is ready to embrace a new future in Love, Alaska—restoring the gift shop she's inherited in time for Christmas. But she gets a blast from the past when childhood pal Finn O'Rourke offers help. With both of them working together, will love become the most unexpected holiday gift of all?

MOUNTAIN COUNTRY COWBOY
Hearts of Hunter Ridge • by Glynna Kaye

For cowboy Cash Herrera, taking a job at Hunter's Hideaway ranch is a chance to gain custody of his son—and work for lovely Rio Hunter. Rio knows the secret she's keeping means leaving Hunter Ridge. But spending time with Cash and his little boy has her wishing for a home with the man who's claiming her heart.

MENDING THE WIDOW'S HEART
Liberty Creek • by Mia Ross

From her first meeting with Sam Calhoun, military widow and single mom Holly Andrews feels a surprising kinship. But she's not looking for permanence. Working on a youth baseball league together rekindles dreams Sam had all but abandoned. Can he convince Holly to stay in Liberty Creek, with him, forever?

A BABY FOR THE DOCTOR
Family Blessings • by Stephanie Dees

Jordan Conley knows Dr. Ash Sheehan would be a perfect pediatrician for her new foster son—but her heart-pounding crush on the confirmed bachelor complicates things. Besides, she's horses and hay, and he's fancy suits. But the more involved he gets in their lives, the more she wishes they could stay together...always.

LICNM0917

Get 2 Free Books,
Plus 2 Free Gifts—
just for trying the
Reader Service!

Love Inspired®

**Inspirational Romance to
Warm Your Heart and Soul**

Join our social communities to connect
with other readers who share your love!

Sign up for the Love Inspired newsletter
at **www.LoveInspired.com** to be the
first to find out about upcoming titles,
special promotions and exclusive content.

CONNECT WITH US AT:

Harlequin.com/Community

 Facebook.com/LoveInspiredBooks

 Twitter.com/LoveInspiredBks